The Silence in Noise and Other Stories

Linda Cassidy Lewis

Published by Two-Four-Six Publishing, 2017.

Also by Linda Cassidy Lewis

A Bay of Dreams Novel
The Brevity of Roses
An Illusion of Trust

A High Tea & Flip-Flops Novel
High Tea & Flip-Flops
Love & Liability
Open & Honest (Sometimes)

Edgewater Love Series
Building Love
Midnight Love

Standalone
The Silence in Noise and Other Stories

Watch for more at https://lindacassidylewis.com.

Table of Contents

For Allen. Always.

Mama's carried a stone in her pocket since she was a child. "For balance," she says. As she grew, so did the size of the stone. The one she carries now, as big as a goose egg and the same shape, has a good heft. It nestles in the palm of her hand so her fingers curve around it perfectly, like God fashioned it just for her. Could be he did, though some folks say it must have been the Devil.

Mama was born with a curve to her spine. It makes her right shoulder sag some and her torso twist a bit in that direction. She don't much kowtow to it, but when she's tired or sick it tends to pull at her more. She carries that stone as a counterweight. It's not enough to straighten her spine; it's just enough to remind her to stand straighter, to fight her weakness.

"That's all there is to it," she tells any stranger who asks her about the stone.

But Janie, Lucy Ann, and me know different.

Sometimes, when the whole family's sitting on the porch, maybe snapping string beans for supper or trying to catch a breeze of a hot summer evening, Mama will slip her hand into her pocket and let her eyes go all sad and far away. We pretend not to notice, and Janie, who likes to laugh as much as breathe, will commence to telling one of her stories. Likely, it's one we've all heard forward and backward, but that don't matter. We carry on like we're in church, except we're laughing.

"Tell it, Sister," we say. "Amen."

Sooner or later, we hear Mama's laughter mingle with ours, and then we relax. I might steal glances at Janie and Lucy Ann, but there's no need for words to pass between us. We know where Mama's mind goes to when she drifts off like that.

Born a year after me, Janie's the second oldest, and Lucy Ann's two years younger than her. We're the only ones old enough to remember what our life was really like when our father lived here. Billy'd just turned six, Penny wasn't three yet, and Tommy Joe was only fourteen months old when Daddy left us. Ten years later, it's still just Mama and the six of us in this house. We had a brother, James Junior, born between Lucy Ann and Billy. He died from a broken neck when he fell from the tree house Daddy'd built him in the pin oak out back. If he'd lived ten days longer, he'd have seen his eighth birthday.

Daddy changed after Jimmy Junior passed.

I have a good memory of Daddy that comforts me some when I'm low. I close my eyes and see him with his hat pulled down so far it's bending his ears in two and covering most of his eyes. His lips are all pooched out and he's chasing Mama around the kitchen for a kiss. She's giggling, her face pink and shiny.

"Patsy, you just dreamed that up," Janie said when I told her once. But I know it happened for real. That was before Daddy's dark time. He used to be a card, just like Janie, but she don't like me saying that. It scares her to think she could turn out like him.

• • • •

I'd just turned twelve when Daddy first took to drink. Mama wasn't happy about that because the church don't approve, but Daddy never much went to church with us anyway. He kept his liquor out of the house and, at first, we never saw him come home drunk. But sometimes me and Janie and Lucy Ann heard him, stumbling up the steps in the dark and swearing at Mama like it was all her fault. We'd lie in our bed, barely breathing.

"Hush," I'd say when I heard them sniffle, "crying don't do no good." But Mama cried when she thought no one was around.

Once that devil got ahold of Daddy, all the tears in the world couldn't have washed it loose. I believe Daddy knew that. You could see it in his eyes when he sat at the supper table after he'd eaten his last bite. He'd stare at his plate for a good while, and when he looked up, his eyes were so sad it like to broke my heart. He looked tuckered out, like he wanted to climb in his bed and not get up for a month of Sundays.

Instead, he'd say, "I believe I'll be going out for a while."

"Bring me some candy," little Billy might say, and Penny'd chime in, "Me too, Daddy." They'd run behind him to the door, but me and Janie and Lucy Ann stayed put. Mama'd lift Tommy Joe from his high-chair and squeeze him close, rocking back and forth in her chair while he squirmed in protest and tears welled up in her eyes.

On those nights, me and the girls cleared the table and washed the dishes. We didn't talk much. After a while, Mama'd carry Tommy Joe from the kitchen and see to getting all the little ones ready for bed. Then we older girls watched TV with her, keeping her company. Eventually, Lucy Ann drifted off, and not long after, Janie slumped against her.

"You girls get to bed now," Mama'd say. "I'm fixing to turn in myself."

That was our life for the next two years. As Daddy's *going out* increased, Mama pulled inward till there wasn't much of her old self visible. Her eyes sunk in like they couldn't bear to see any more of life. Even though she dropped that stone into her pocket every morning, Mama no longer tried to stand up straight. A slumped and twisted scarecrow with stringy hair and sharp collarbones hid our beautiful Mama.

As Daddy got sicker, he more than cursed her when he staggered in. He threw things. He slapped and kicked and pinched her hard enough to leave bruises. She hid the marks when she could, but enough peeked through her hair and below her sleeves or hem to break my heart. More than once, long past midnight, he dragged her out of bed and forced her down to the kitchen to fix him a meal. On the nights Daddy went out, I slept light, my eyes flying open at the first sound of his return. I took to creeping down the stairs after them, trying to steel myself to take his blows if they were too much for Mama.

On that last night, Daddy came home before Mama turned off the TV. She'd just shooed us girls up the stairs, but we froze at the top when we heard his boots clomp across the porch boards. Daddy'd been gone from the house for more than twenty-four hours.

"You two go on up and stay there," I whispered to Janie and Lucy Ann. "This is going to be bad. If the little ones wake up, make sure they don't come downstairs." I tiptoed back down and stood on the bottom step, out of sight, listening.

"Where's my supper, Mary Beth?" Daddy's growl sent a shiver through me. Tears of longing, like homesickness, welled in my eyes. My real Daddy was gone forever.

"Shush, Jimmy. The kids are sleeping. Come on."

I waited a minute before following them. I could see the kitchen window from where I crouched outside the open door. The night's darkness behind the glass made it like a mirror, reflecting Daddy sitting at the table, his head propped in his hands. Mama stood at the stove, heating the iron skillet. When she turned and headed to the refrigerator, I ducked back and squashed Janie and Lucy Ann who'd crept up without me knowing. I didn't dare say a word for fear Daddy'd hear, but I cut my eyes at them something fierce.

Daddy's mumbling drew my attention back to the kitchen. "Sorry. . . . so sorry . . . told him . . . sorry . . ." He threw his arms wide. " . . . persecuting me!" His chair scraped on the linoleum, and then he stepped into view. I ducked back again, even though he faced away from me. "Damn them!"

I prayed his raging wouldn't wake up the little ones. I dared a peek. He was pacing, his hands beating at the air.

"It's you that done it." He grabbed his head and groaned. "God, help me. There's fish in my brain."

He dropped back into his chair and sat quiet for a moment, watching Mama work. "I wish you'd stopped me from building that damned tree house, Mary Beth." He shook his head, slow and sad. Thirty seconds later, he shot to his feet and began pacing again. "Look at this. Look! Damned witches . . . poison . . ." He stopped and whipped his head toward the window, staring for a minute before he yelled. "Hell fire, Granddaddy!" He laughed, a high-pitched crazy sound.

The girls latched on to me, trembling. Daddy swung in and out of my view as he walked the floor, still mumbling and yelling.

"Liars! They're behind it all!"

We girls jumped when something crashed against the opposite side of the wall where we crouched. Drops of some liquid and a shard of glass flew through the open doorway, landing inches from my toes.

"Sit down, Jimmy," Mama said. "Your eggs are almost done."

How could she sound so calm? Had the worst passed? I sighed, and the girls relaxed their hold on my shirt. We sat side by side, staring ahead. I listened for the sound of the chair scooting back up to the table. Every second of silence wound me up tighter.

"*What did you say?*" Daddy's voice didn't even sound human.

I don't remember jumping up. I never felt the glass slicing the ball of my foot. All I know is, suddenly we girls were in the kitchen. Lucy Ann ran toward Mama but froze when she caught site of Daddy's face, twisted up in rage, his soft brown eyes turned black as tar.

Mama, who stood facing Daddy, flicked her eyes sideways at the hot pan. Both me and Janie caught her plea, but Janie moved quicker. She ran to the stove, cut the flame, grabbed the pan, and dropped it into the sink. She held her scorched hand in the cold stream running to cool down the pan Daddy might have used as a weapon. The sight of Mama watching him like a trapped raccoon with no hope of escape chilled my blood.

I pulled Lucy Ann back as I moved closer to Daddy. If Mama wouldn't fight him, I would. He gave no sign that he saw anyone in the room but Mama—if, in his madness, she was really who he saw. The low rumble that rose from Daddy's chest grew to a roar as he lunged. He flew past me before I could react. A trio of screams rose from us girls as

Daddy's hands closed on Mama's neck. He lifted her till only her toes scrabbled on the linoleum. The girls shrieked for me to help her, but before I could move, Mama's arm cut an arc through the air. Once. Twice. Again. Again.

Daddy's hands lost their grip and she fell back against the stove as he slumped to the floor. My eyes fixed on the bloody stone gripped in Mama's hand. For a time, no one moved.

Mama stared straight ahead, her mouth slack, her eyes empty.

Janie stared where Daddy'd fallen.

Tears streamed down Lucy Ann's face.

I grabbed her arm. "Take Mama on out of here, Lucy Ann."

Janie looked up at me. "What are we going to do with—"

"He didn't come home tonight. That's what we're all going to tell the sheriff. Understand? We'll say, ain't none of us seen him since supper on Tuesday. Lucy Ann, make sure Mama knows what to say, you hear?"

I waited until she led Mama out of the kitchen, and then I motioned to Janie. "Grab his feet."

Janie and I dragged Daddy's body out the kitchen door and along the porch to the front. We left him with his wounded head lying against the bottom step and then cleaned up the blood left behind. Blood from his wound. Blood from my cut foot. Mingled on the porch and in the kitchen and in my conscience.

We called the sheriff at the first glow of dawn, before the little ones woke up. Sheriff Warren's a smart man, but he studied on how tore up Mama was and didn't ask too many questions. Folks around here take care of their own.

• • • •

We're all haunted by that night, but Mama's got it the worst. Some of Daddy's kin guess the truth and talk evil of her, but they ain't from around here. They didn't see how grief and drink took Daddy away long before that night. I say they ought not let their high and mighty morals trump common decency and justice. Mama did what she had to do to bring our life back into balance. The townsfolk understand and treat us kindly, but a big part of Mama went with Daddy. That's why I'll stay here till the end for her. And Janie might too.

She and I still don't sleep well. I believe, at some point on most nights, we're lying in the dark listening for the sound of boot steps clomping across the porch. The two of us never talk about what we heard that night as we walked away from the steps.

A moan. Daddy's moan.

I wake in a house that is not mine. I am not home, yet I am not a stranger in this house. I arrived here just after sunset, *Tapestry* playing on my new 8-track player, exhausted from driving straight through because I couldn't stand to see Russell again. I'd called ahead; my in-laws knew their son was not coming with me. I sensed their relief. No questions asked. They welcomed me, fed me, and sent me off to bed.

Now, hours later, I lie here, warm beneath a faded quilt, morning birdsong drifting through the open window. The cross-stitched sampler hanging on a wall of this room proclaims a sentiment I long to feel: Home Sweet Home.

I stretch and breathe deeply. With nose and imagination, I count the scents of a waiting breakfast—fried bacon, biscuits, cream gravy, eggs, and blackberry jam. My watering mouth draws me up from the mattress, swayed from the weight of the countless bodies that have slept in this guest room. Evidently, under the circumstances, my mother-in-law, Libby, felt it would be in poor taste to put me up in Russell's old room.

Nestled in a spot in Kentucky known as Slate Hollow—Slate Holler, they say here—this house has remained in Russell's family for generations. These nine rooms grew from the one-room cabin built by his ancestor over one hundred and fifty years ago. Indoor plumbing is a relatively new addition, and the only bathroom is downstairs. Before heading that way, I pull on a peasant top and my new bell-bottomed jeans, then drag a comb through my tangled auburn curls and wrangle them into a ponytail.

When I walk into the kitchen minutes later, Libby jumps up from her chair at one end of the table and moves to the stove. Russell's father, Frank, his sister Arlene, and the hired man, Jesse, have nearly finished eating. I make a mental note to wake myself earlier tomorrow.

As usual, Libby has delayed her breakfast. Nothing persuades her to eat before she serves all others. Nothing will dissuade her from frying my eggs to order. She asks my preference with a look.

"Just one, over easy, please." I pour a cup of coffee and take a seat at the table. With an oft-present twinkle in his eyes, Frank smiles and nods good morning. He's not a talker, though he puts to shame Jesse, who hasn't even looked up from his plate.

Arlene takes up the slack for both. "How'd you sleep, Nicole?"

"Very well, thank you."

She makes a face. "In that old bed? I can't imagine you did. If Robert E. Lee ever roamed this far north into Kentucky, I expect he slept on that same mattress."

"Now, Arlene . . ." Libby says.

"Oh Mama, you know that's almost true. Nothing ever changes around here. If it's not broken, it's not going be replaced. And even if it is broken, it might be years before we get a new one."

Libby sighs.

Frank keeps his head down. He isolates himself from Arlene's constant complaining as a way to preserve his positive outlook.

Though she, his youngest daughter, works in the paper mill outside of town, she's apt to call-in sick at the slightest provocation, and spends her resultant meager paycheck on what he would call frippery rather than contribute to the household fund for purchasing any of the broken or worn out items she laments. At twenty-six, Arlene is still a child.

At thirty-two, is Russell any more mature?

Libby sets a plate before me and, at last, returns to the stove to fix her own. I know the workings of this family, not from Russell, but from Libby, who is surprisingly forthcoming, more so in the letters she writes to me than in our conversations. Though often mute in the company of others, she transforms the second she puts pen to paper. It's to this other side of Libby I feel free to confess my problems with her son.

Russell never understood my correspondence with his mother, but if not for that, I would know very little about his family. He brought me here once soon after we married and less than a dozen more times in the six years since. I don't remember him ever initiating a phone conversation with either of his parents, and many times, when I answered their calls, he signaled for me to tell them he wasn't home.

Even the name he chooses to go by turns its back on his family. He was born John Russell Conway and called Johnny for the first twenty-four years of his life, but—so he says—when he scraped that hillbilly mud off his shoes and moved north to Indianapolis, he became a new man.

He did not become a better man.

Arlene gets up, pours herself another cup of coffee, and then glances at the clock. "Oh, now look at that. I'm going to be late to work." As usual, her voice has settled in the groove between whine and fret. "Why didn't you tell me, Mama? I bet the girls have been honking their horn out there forever. What will they think of me?" She dumps her coffee down the sink. "I guess I'll just have to start eating my breakfast on the porch so I can see when their car pulls up."

"Now, Arlene, don't work yourself up." Libby directs this advice toward her daughter's back because Arlene's already on her way to the front door.

Frank breathes a weary sigh.

Libby sets her plate on the table and pours herself what's left of the coffee—a scant two-thirds cup. Surely, to herself, she must curse her daughter's selfishness, but there's no trace of it in her expression as she takes her place at the table.

For a few minutes, only metallic scrapes on china and quiet slurps of hot coffee interrupt the silence. My thoughts wander to Russell. What would he be doing right now? This early in the morning, is he even conscious? I glance at the electric clock hung on the wall behind Jesse, its plastic case and cord yellowed with age. Right now, if I were home, I'd be in my classroom preparing for summer school to start next week. I *should* be in my classroom. Why did I run away? I could have stayed and just left the house on Saturday to avoid seeing Russell. Am I a coward?

Frank and Jesse rise at the same time as though attuned to an alarm I cannot hear.

"We have tobacco to tend to," Frank says. He and Jesse scoot their chairs back under the table. "Nicole," Frank says and nods his good-bye.

Jesse mimes his movement, though he might well have been nodding at the table since his eyes never rose above my hands.

"Mama." Frank winks and tips his head in Libby's direction.

I marvel that so much can be said with just a word and gesture between two people who've built a life together, a couple whose love has grown deeper with each passing year. A couple unlike Russell and I will ever be.

The men leave through the door to the screened porch connecting the house to the original cabin, which is now Jesse's room. The family calls this porch the summer kitchen, though I doubt anyone has used the cast iron cook stove in decades, and a stew of dusty canning jars, gathering baskets, and chipped enameled pots nearly hides the table. Only the old pump sink in the room gets regular use, by the women to rinse off vegetables from the garden and by the men to wash their dirty hands and cool their sweaty faces and necks when they come in from the fields.

"Since I'm here to help with your work," I tell Libby, "you can take a little time to sit this morning." Then, without asking because I know she will take on the task herself, I get up and start making another pot of coffee. The avocado green electric percolator stands out, oddly modern, in this kitchen with its decades old wallpaper and furnishings that are now antique.

Behind me, Libby sighs deeply, as though grateful someone has finally granted her permission to relax. I glance over my shoulder. She's sitting with her hands folded, eyes closed, a slight smile dimpling her face. As in her letter writing, Libby is a different person, she is herself, when not in the presence of men. This life of deference, this relic of the past, is not one I was raised to, and for a moment, I wonder if my boldness is the cause of problems between Russell and me.

Then, I remember.

Two days ago, I faced reality. Six years have passed since Russell and I married. We've been saving to buy our dream home. No. Let's tell it like it is. I saved. I dreamed. Russell had secrets. He had another plan. Or no plan, as it turned out. He had excuses. It wasn't his fault the time sheet got screwed up, and they shorted him on his paycheck. It wasn't his fault the guys at work were offended if he didn't go out for drinks with them after work two or three nights a week. It wasn't his fault the sales manager sent him off to the middle of nowhere to deliver a car, leaving him too tired to drive home Sunday night.

But I'd followed him on Sunday when he said he needed to go in to work for a while. He'd never worked on a Sunday before. He didn't work that Sunday either. He drove to Brookside Apartments. I watched him knock on a faded green door and then walk into the arms of another woman. She was the *real* reason he didn't come home until breakfast.

So while Russell sprawled, half asleep and fully oblivious, on the living room couch, I stood in our bedroom and faced the truth about my marriage. It didn't exist. The certificate saying it did remained in our file cabinet. Our wedding photo still sat right there on my chest of drawers. But the relationship they proclaimed had dissolved.

Resigned, I began filling a duffel bag with his clothes. Twice, I stopped. One of those times, I even pulled some things back out, but despite the fear roiling in my stomach, I put them back and carried the bag into the living room.

"Get out," I told him, heaving the bag at him. "If you need to get in touch with me—which you shouldn't—call me."

"What the hell?" Russell knocked the duffel to the floor as he struggled to get to his feet. "Just hold on. I'm not going anywhere. This is my house too."

"Really? I believe the lease is in my name only—"

"You had a better credit history."

"I'm sick of supporting you, Russell."

"No one supports me. I have a job."

"For now."

"And what's that supposed to mean?"

"How often is your mind clear enough to remember that job and drag your sorry ass down there?"

He turned toward me, eyes flashing, and despite my resolve not to let him intimidate me this time, I backed up a step.

"If you had ever, for one second, climbed down off your high horse," he said, "I wouldn't have had to look for an escape."

"You're blaming *me*? It's *my* fault you're an addict?"

"Don't you—" He stepped forward, his fist pulled back. Then he took a deep breath and unclenched his hand. "I am *not* an addict." He backed up and slumped down on the couch. He leaned forward, resting his elbows on his knees, and threaded his fingers through his hair. "Look, I know I've screwed up, but let's just talk about this, okay?"

"Let's just talk about all the things that have gone missing from this house in the last few months, Russell. The jewelry my mother left me, my great-grandmother's silver tea service, our stereo, *two* TVs, and—"

"We've had break-ins, Nicole. You know that."

"Funny how those break-ins always occur in the middle of the day when *I'm* at work."

He kicked the duffel but then sat still. After a moment, he looked up at me like a child still hoping to talk his way out of punishment. "Where am I supposed to go, Nik?"

I took a deep breath. I could do this. "Why not move in with your scummy girlfriend?" Surprise lit his glance before it darkened to a glare. He thought he'd kept that secret from me. "Let *her* support your habit."

Russell grabbed his shoes, shoved his feet into them, and stood. He looked hard at me for a moment and then, with a sneer, shook his head as if he pitied me. "You know what your problem is? You can't stand to share your life with anyone who doesn't live strictly by the Rules of Nicole. Well, good luck with your lifetime of loneliness, sweetheart." He picked up the bag and slung the strap over his shoulder. "I'll be back for the rest of my stuff this weekend." He opened the door and then flashed me one of his phony customer service smiles. "Have a nice day."

Now, when the pot signals the coffee is ready, I fill Libby's cup and mine and carry them back to the table. She rouses from her daydream.

"Do you think Russell will follow you here?" she asks.

"No." I place Libby's cup before her and sit back down. She knows about Russell's alcoholism and drug use, but should I tell her the rest? How much detail is necessary to explain why Russell and I have separated? Maybe it would be kinder to keep the details to myself. Or am I just reluctant to reveal my final humiliation? "Actually, I don't know." I shake my head. "I'm not thinking clearly."

"You said last night that you needed to chill for a while."

My laugh is weak. "I said *chill*?"

"Why now, Nicole?"

I only look at her.

"Has something happened? Something more than the liquor and pills?"

I search her eyes. Does she know already? I breathe deeply and let it go. "Russell has a girlfriend." My face burns as if that admission were a slap.

"Is he leaving you?"

Libby's asking if Russell is moving his body out of our house, so I answer, "Yes." I take no offense that my ordering Russell to leave doesn't occur to her. To her way of thinking, to her generation, a woman doesn't have that right. "He left yesterday morning." In truth, he left me long ago. "And he's moving his things out this weekend. That's why I came here."

"But what if he . . . he could take more than just his things." With fingers beginning to gnarl with arthritis, she twists her coffee cup one way and then back again. "You said he's sold things before . . . to get money to buy . . ."

"There's nothing much left, Libby. What was valuable to me, I brought with me."

She looks at me, her eyes alight. "What will you do, now?"

I shrug. After all that's happened in the last year, how can I not have come up with a plan? But I know why; I never thought I'd find the courage to leave.

"You're more than welcome to stay here, Nicole."

"Stay?" That unlikely thought lights a wick of hope.

She nods. "For as long as you want."

I know she means that, and the invitation is everlasting, but I wonder why. Does she welcome me because I am loved for myself, or does she offer out of a sense of duty, as an apology for birthing a son who has turned out to be a disappointment to us both?

. . . .

Libby and I rest on the porch for a few minutes between morning's work and dinner preparations. She dozes in her rocker, and I watch the honeybees buzz the wisteria over the front stepstones. Libby's grandmother planted that vine. I sit in awe of the permanence of life here. Nothing has ever been permanent in my life. Libby's children are the sixth generation born in this house. In a past era, as first-born son, the house and land would have been Russell's inheritance, but Frank and Libby will divide it equally between their three children. That is, if Russell doesn't overdose and die before his parents.

Is it strange that Libby should invite me to stay here, as though I'm a changeling, a good substitute for a child gone bad? What would I do if I stayed? Where is the nearest school, and would they hire me to teach? God forbid, I'd have to drive very far on these twisted country roads. I swear I held my breath the last twenty minutes of the drive here.

"We best get dinner on the table," Libby says, startling me for the second time today. Her circadian rhythm, long tuned to the quality of light throughout the day, guides her whether she's awake or asleep.

While Libby lays out cold ham, sliced tomatoes with onions, and potato salad for dinner, which is what they call the noon meal here, I go to the garden behind the house to pick green beans for supper. I ring the cast iron dinner bell, more for the thrill than necessity. Frank and Jesse, by the sun's position as much as their watches, would come in from the field without the signal. I open the gate and kick off my sandals on the way in. I love the feel of warm soil squished between my toes. As I pass by, I brush my hand over the tomato plants to release their scent and breathe it in. I pick the pole beans. On the way back out, I pop a yellow cherry tomato, still hot from the sun, into my mouth. Sweet and acidic, the flavor bursts in my mouth like a secret elixir.

All things are more alive here.

The men are washing up when I enter the summer porch with my basket, so I carry it into the kitchen and set it on the Hoosier cabinet. I imagine it's stood in this corner for generations. How many women have rolled out their biscuit dough on that cool porcelain surface?

We take our seats and pass the dishes around the table, serving ourselves. We eat without speaking for a few minutes. The silence reminds me of the tension I've been living under at home, so I break it to inquire about Russell's married sister. "How are Carla and Jimmy doing?"

"Right well," Frank says.

Because it's Frank answering, I don't know if this means things truly are well, or he's making the best of the whole family being down with some plague. I look to Libby for a translation.

"Jimmy got promoted at the mill," she says, "and Carla's got another baby coming."

"Four children. That's wonderful," I say, and then the realization I may never be a mother strangles me. But do I really want to be? What of that parents' guilt Libby's expressed? I could give birth to a son that, for the rest of my life, I felt a need to apologize for. A son like Russell.

Frank and Jesse discuss some repairs needed to the curing barn, and as I listen, I wonder if Frank thinks of Jesse as the son Russell should have been. Would Frank have gladly chosen this awkward, shaggy-haired man over his gregarious, handsome flesh and blood? Did he try but fail to guide his son down the right path, or did he see the destruction that lay ahead and turn his twinkling eyes away? But then, how dare I judge him, or Libby, when I didn't foresee what Russell would become?

Too soon, the midday meal is over, and the men rise to return to their work. Again, the nicety of nods is exchanged, only this time Jesse's gaze lands somewhere in the vicinity of my chin. Progress. In the six years I've known him, he's never once seemed comfortable in my presence. He's a mystery. What would it be like to have a real conversation with him? When I do catch a glimpse of his blue eyes, they hint at a lively mind behind them.

Libby makes an announcement as we finish washing the dinner dishes. "I've got half a mind to fry up some chicken for supper."

"I'll snap the beans," I say. She gives me a knowing smile. The first time Russell brought me here, I followed Libby to the chicken yard, ignorant of exactly what I had volunteered for. She strode several steps ahead of me. I passed a kettle set to boil over a fire in the yard and was about to ask for what, when she snatched up a hen and started back toward me. I watched in horror as she took it by the neck, swung it in a circle, slammed it down on the wood block, and chopped off its head. With the stench of blood and wet feathers lingering in my nose, I let the chicken platter pass me by that day. Though I still decline to participate in the beginning of the process, I've overcome my aversion to the end product.

• • • •

We have come to sit on the porch after supper, a meal during which Jesse looked directly at me once, though judging by the crimson hue that rose to his ears, he didn't mean for me to catch him. As I imagine they have since the day they married, Frank and Libby sit side-by-side in caned rockers. I sit beside them. Arlene perches on the porch edge in front of us, facing away. Jesse settles on the far edge, off to the side, smoking. He leans back against a post with one leg extended before him and the other bent, his foot resting on the ground.

At the end of this long, summer day, the scents of mown grass and honeysuckle blend with a hint of sun-warmed tar from the road beyond the gate and waft around us. For a few silent moments, we sit and breathe and watch as the setting sun reddens the world. Then, at the dimming of the light, the air comes alive with sounds of country night life.

"What bird is that calling?" I ask.

"Whippoorwill," Arlene says.

Frank points. "Up yonder sits a bobwhite. Listen for him."

I do. I hear it call out its name. The sights and sounds and scents lull me. Even Arlene is hushed. I sit as if dreaming, not wanting to move lest I wake.

Frank says, "If you've a mind to, Nicole, you could drive Libby into town tomorrow evening. She wants to go to a special meeting of the local church ladies."

"Well, I'm going too, then," Arlene says.

Libby speaks up, "Now, Arlene, Nicole didn't say she wants—"

"Yes," I say, "I'll take you." Then I add, "I hope the road isn't treacherous curves the whole way though. I didn't do too well driving down here."

"Aw, tain't nothing once you learn the secret," Jesse says.

For a second, I'm mute from surprise that Jesse spoke to me. "The secret?"

"Yes'm, you hug in close when you enter a turn, then shoot straight for a ways, edging out to the op'site side. You just straighten out them curves, you be all right."

Jesse drops his gaze quickly, though whether it's because he spoke to me or spoke at all, I can't tell. It may be the first time he's addressed me voluntarily. He's certainly never shared a more intimate opinion with me.

"Thank you, Jesse. I'll remember that."

We grow quiet again. As twilight deepens, night slides down into this hollow. The insect symphony rises to a crescendo. The others excuse themselves for bed, but I linger, gazing blindly into honest darkness and listening to the sounds of life around me. There is peace in this place of work and reward, early sleep and waking. There is hope.

I lie to myself. I think I knew from the start that Russell was a man who would never be true to me, a tawny lion who could never be tamed. My pride held on while he spun in ever-widening circles. In his heart, he left me after two years; it took me four more to leave him.

The night touches me with soft kisses, its promises true, devoutly kept. I breathe it in and exhale pain and fear. I rise and enter the house, fumbling for the door lock out of habit. I pause. In this place, there's no need to lock anyone out. I am safe here. If I can learn to *straighten out them curves*, I will be all right.

Through the open window, I watch Josh and Teddy playing on the lush summer grass. Head to head, Josh's thick chestnut curls entwine with Teddy's baby-fine golden ones. Father and son. Inseparable.

A warm breeze carries to me the sweet scent of jasmine mingled with their voices. Breathe. I jerk the now-silent phone away from my ear. I switch it off. Lock it. Set it down on the table beside me and shove it to the far side. I won't tell Josh today. I want to never tell him.

Test positive. Malignant. Inoperable. How can I say those unspeakable words to him?

I am sculpted in ice, transparent in the sunlight streaming through the window. Josh, straddling his son across his stomach, lies on his back to begin another game. How will he receive such cruel news? My husband, so young, so strong. But not invincible.

I am growing numb, as though a part of me knew the test results before the call and started preparations. Started recording the sequence of events to come on my mental calendar and programming my responses. A merciful detachment already in progress.

When Josh sits up and glances toward the house, I retreat from the window. Shadow sliding into shadow. "Where's Mommy?" he asks our son. He will stand now, lifting Teddy to his shoulders, and he will come to me laughing, carefree, blissful in ignorance.

As if the world has no end.

As if no evil thing that wraps around your brain and sucks the life out of it exists.

As if our beautiful son will be with us forever.

James was a man at the top of his game. After two months of planning down to the last detail, he had pulled it off, and now, so jazzed he could hardly stand still, he grinned at himself in the mirrored walls of the elevator. Damn, he looked good! Thirty-two years had chiseled his face to near perfection, and all those hours at the health club had worked magic on his body. As the elevator reached the floor of Ann's Tribeca loft, he gave his reflection a thumbs-up.

He unlocked the door and stepped inside, careful to slip off his shoes in the entryway. If he didn't, Ann would bitch about wear on her Brazilian walnut floors and cashmere rugs, though that concern never stopped her from pacing them when angry or anxious, like she'd been this morning before he left for the airport.

He headed straight for their bedroom where she'd be waiting with a chilled bottle of Cristal, ready to celebrate his return. It disappointed him—annoyed him, really—to find she'd dozed off. Despite that, he couldn't help admiring the way her hair lay in waves against the ivory silk pillowcase, an ebony frame for her porcelain face. She looked as delicate as a hummingbird. Ann was as beautiful as she was smart but not nearly as tough as she thought. She had let herself fall for him.

James set his briefcase beside the bed and reached for the bottle. When he popped the cork, Ann woke. Her eyes flew open and darted wildly for a second before lighting on him. She smiled then and sat up.

"So?" she said.

He poured two flutes of champagne and handed one to her. For a moment, he wore his face as a mask, then their eyes locked, and he broke into a grin. "Easy as pie."

"You're amazing!" She raised her glass in a toast.

"It was all your planning, babe. You're the brains of this team; I'm just the brawn."

"Essential as that is"—Ann set aside her champagne and reached to pull him down to her—"it's not all you're good for, you beautiful man."

• • • •

At ten o'clock the next morning, Ann sent James out for coffee. He ordered her mocha and his house blend, then studied the other patrons while he waited. They were the usual crew: students, white-collar types, teen-aged girls, and shopaholic wives. Just as the barista finished his order, James spotted the redhead weeping in the corner. A gorgeous woman, even with a tear-stained face, and, if the Louboutin pumps on her feet and the Prada bag she rummaged through were evidence, possibly rich. He grabbed the cups along with a napkin and headed for her table.

"Here you go, not exactly the finest linen, but . . ."

"Thank you." She took the napkin with a delicate hand—heavy with diamonds—and blotted her tears.

James set one cup in front of her. "Looks like you could use this too."

"Oh, no, I couldn't . . ."

"Please," he said. "It's my good deed for the day." With a wink, he sat his cup on the table and took the chair opposite hers.

She tasted the mocha. "I'm sorry. Believe it or not, I hate public displays of emotion like this."

"I try to limit mine to once a week." He grinned at her, and she smiled in spite of her tears. "I'm James."

"Lauren." She pressed two perfectly manicured fingers to her lips as if to stifle a sob.

"Now, now, what's got you so upset this beautiful morning?"

"My husband is divorcing me. My lying, cheating, scumbag of a husband." She sniffed, then gave him a weak smile. "So why am I crying?"

"Good question. Why *are* you crying?"

Lauren took two sips before answering. "I actually thought he loved me. Instead, he *humiliated* me. This morning, he tells me he's moving in with his girlfriend, but that's only temporary because his lawyer will make sure he gets *everything*. So I'm standing there in shock, and he says, 'You might as well make this easier and just run back home to West Virginia. There won't be anything left for you here."

James furrowed his brow. "Scumbag is too good a word for a guy like that."

"True."

"So . . . *are* you going back to West Virginia?"

"No, *please*, anything but that. I worked too hard to get away from there."

James nodded in sympathy. He knew that I'll-die-if-I-don't-get-out-of-here feeling all too well. Sometimes, he could swear the sound of his mama and granny wailing for Jesus to save his blackened soul woke him in the middle of the night. "Well then," he told her, "you need a better lawyer than he has."

"Oh, I have one." Lauren gave him a full-blown smile. I retained mine before we married." She blotted away the last of her tears. "So it won't be *me* left with nothing. He'll be living with that little whore for longer than he thinks." She laughed. "Maybe I'll send the two of *them* tickets to West Virginia."

"Revenge is sweet," James said.

"So are you."

"Nah, I just have a weakness for pretty ladies in need of a little help."

Lauren studied him for a moment. Then, her eyes lit up. "Is that so? Well, if you *really* wanted to help me out, I could think of something better than a cup of coffee and sympathy."

James grinned. "And what would that be?"

She gazed into his eyes and slowly traced her lips with the tip of her tongue as she trailed her long nails along his hand. "You could," she said, "try to make me believe that a gorgeous hunk like you finds me desirable."

"That's definitely something I could do. And I wouldn't have to fake it."

"Well, well, did I mention I live right around the corner?"

"Imagine that," James said just as a text alert sounded on his cell phone. He read the message. "Damn, wouldn't you know. I've been waiting to hear from this client for a week, and now he wants to meet with me this morning."

Lauren narrowed her eyes. "Or maybe you're having second thoughts?"

"Now, what kind of fool would do that?" He flashed another grin. "Look, I'll be free later this afternoon, so let's continue this conversation then." James stood and offered Lauren his arm. "Right now, let me act the gentleman and walk you home."

He hoped Lauren would turn left when they stepped out of the coffee house, but she didn't. When their walk ended two blocks later, he silently cursed his bad luck. Lauren had stopped in front of Ann's building. His only break was that Ann wouldn't have seen them arrive together because her apartment overlooked the main entrance, around the corner.

"This is it," Lauren announced.

"Uh, yeah, nice place. I had a friend who lived here."

"Oh?"

"You know, just in case this client turns out to need hand-holding all day, why don't you give me your number?" He smiled. "I wouldn't want you to think I stood you up."

Lauren produced a monogrammed card out of her purse and slipped it into his back pocket. "Don't keep me waiting too long, love. I don't know how much anticipation I can stand."

"It's a promise." He held open the lobby door, then watched until the elevator doors closed behind her before sprinting back to order another mocha for Ann. He was about to play a dangerous game. But then, without danger, where was the thrill?

• • • •

"Sorry about that, babe." James handed the mocha to Ann. "I ran into some guy I used to know."

Ann studied him for a moment. "You didn't respond to my text."

"Yeah, I know, but it gave me the excuse to tell him I had to go. Hey, if you don't have plans for me this afternoon, I think I'll spend a little time in the gym. Need to keep in shape for the next job."

"Take all the time you want," she said, smiling. "I'll do some shopping. I might even meet a friend for dinner. You can fend for yourself, can't you?"

"Don't worry about me," he said. "I'll do just fine."

Before James phoned Lauren that afternoon, he considered the pros and cons of the situation. With them all living in the same building, he could slip away easier to see Lauren. The flip side was the ever-present chance of an awkward meeting. But then the building's U-shape, wrapped around a central courtyard and pool with entrances off all three sides, might diminish that likelihood. In fact, he had lived here all of March and April but had never seen Lauren once. He would have remembered.

• • • •

For two weeks, James lived in paradise—plenty of money to spend and plenty of sex with two gorgeous women. There was only one complication. His old weakness had crept in. Conscience. He started to feel he owed Ann some loyalty, and he had second thoughts about his plan to scam Lauren out of her money. But he doubled down on his determination to stay strong, to work out those bugs. To get his goddam priorities straight.

Then one morning he woke late. Lying in bed, he listened for sounds of Ann moving around the apartment. He heard only silence. Curious, he roused himself and wandered into the kitchen. Ann's note lay on the counter: *Come down to the pool, sleepyhead.* His hope of a leisurely breakfast dashed, James downed a protein shake and prepared to join her.

He scanned the pool. Then, because Ann claimed the sun gave her too many freckles and not enough tan, he scanned the lounges on the shaded side of it. A familiar laugh caught his ear. He turned toward it and, by reflex, sucked in air that never made it past the invisible fist clenching his throat. Ann and Lauren sat side by side. His brain screamed for him to get the hell out of there, but before he could move, Ann waved him over.

James kept a smile frozen on his face while Ann introduced him to Lauren. He managed a polite nice-to-meet-you, then he dove into the pool. He swam laps. With occasional glances at the two women chatting and laughing, he wondered what they found so damned funny. Though Lauren had played it cool, and he had no reason to think Ann suspected anything, their meeting had forced his hand. He would have to make a choice—and soon.

• • • •

After Ann had fallen asleep that night, James slipped out of their bed. She slept like the dead, seven or eight hours usually. Still, he'd dressed in jogging clothes just in case she woke before he returned and he needed an excuse for his absence. Now, midway between midnight and dawn, he and Lauren lay on her black silk sheets, their bodies ghostly in the moonlight.

Lauren teased a lock of her long hair against his cheek. "What we're feeling isn't wrong, James," she whispered. "There's no reason for you to feel guilty."

"But Ann gave me a new start."

"She *gave* you nothing. She doesn't see you as her partner; you're her employee. You've earned her a bundle, and yet, she makes you feel like her puppet."

"You don't know—"

"Yes, I *do* know. Maybe I don't know what happened to you in the past, why you feel so indebted to her, but I know she's taken advantage of that."

James lay still, eyes fixed on the ceiling. "I guess I *am* pulling my weight," he admitted finally, "but still, she took a chance on me."

Lauren propped herself up on one elbow and laid her hand over his heart. "Oh James, love, she's used your feelings to convince you that you couldn't have made it without her. Trust me; I'm a woman too. I know the games."

He turned his face to hers. Though he had practiced it his whole life, sometimes his acting ability still amazed him. His voice choked as he said, "If only I'd met you first."

"Well, I'm here now. Isn't that enough?"

"But I just don't know how I can tell her it's over." He focused back on the ceiling and sighed deeply. "We're living in the same building, for God's sake. How awkward will that be?"

"Well . . . I've been meaning to tell you . . . I'm going to be moving."

"You're selling this place?"

Lauren paused, tapping out the seconds on his chest with her nails. "Well, not exactly. You see, I sort of misrepresented my situation the day I met you, and then after we . . . well, it got complicated. But I guess it's time to clear something up, considering the circumstances." She trailed her fingertips lightly south. "The truth is, I wasn't actually *married* to Mark. I was more like his mistress."

James drew a sharp breath, but he remained calm—considering the circumstances. "His mistress?"

"Right. So, you see, he's been paying for this place, and now I have to get out because . . . well . . . I don't have any *real* money. I'm kind of on my own now."

Unbelievable! The woman was smiling. He could hear it in her voice.

"On your own," he repeated.

"Well, not exactly. Not anymore. I have you now, love."

"Yes . . . me."

"And *about* you, about Ann, you *have* to leave her. She's like a black widow spider, James. She'll use you as long as she needs you and then . . ." Lauren laid her hand against his cheek, turning his face to hers. She brushed her lips against his as she spoke, "You deserve more, love. I can give you so much more."

• • • •

Less than twenty-four hours later, James sat on the edge of the sofa, ready to defend himself. Physically, if it came to that—this was one furious woman pacing before him. He could almost feel the blood flow every time her eyes pierced him. He had screwed himself royally with his plan to con that stupid bitch Lauren. He couldn't afford to blow off Ann now.

"I can't believe you slept with Lauren."

"Ann, please—"

"You son of a bitch! Practically, right under my roof. You slept with *Lauren.*"

"It means nothing, babe, I swear it."

"It means something to *me*." She stopped in front of him. Loomed over him.

"Look—believe me—I know I made a big mistake, but I swear, it won't happen—"

"She's threatened to go to the police!" Ann told him.

That stopped him cold for a moment. "With what? I mean . . . she doesn't know anything."

"And you know that how? *Pillow talk*?" She closed her eyes for a moment, then continued through clenched teeth, "She has evidence against *me*, James. For something I did on my own . . . *before* I met you."

He had no idea how Lauren could know anything about Ann's past, but he breathed easier knowing he was in the clear. "She won't do anything with the evidence," he said. "Why would she?"

"Because a jealous woman is a dangerous thing, James."

"Jealous?"

"Either I let you go, or she'll bring me down. Did you *hear* me, James? She's not threatening *you*!"

"Babe, I never meant for this to—"

"Really? *Really*. How stupid I was!" She paced again. "Like you suddenly needed to triple your workouts. Like all these long-lost buddies just showed up out of the blue. And don't even *dare* to tell me this had nothing to do with the fact she was soon to be the single and *rich* Lauren!"

James jumped to his feet. "No no *no*! I didn't plan it like that, I swear. You and I are a team. I love you. How could you think otherwise?"

Ann stopped dead and turned toward him, her eyes wide. "Oh God. Now I get it. I'm *such* an idiot. The two of you planned this together, didn't you? I'm a complete *fool*."

"No, no, I swear. I love you, babe. What can I do to prove it to you?"

Ann crossed her arms and stared at him for a full agonizing minute before she answered. "One of us has to be removed from this cozy little *love* triangle, James. And I'm not voting for me . . . or you."

Ann left the apartment after her rant, leaving James alone to make his decision. He stood at the bedroom windows looking toward the Manhattan skyline. If he lived here the rest of his life, he would never feel he belonged. Why not cut his losses and head for the airport right now? He could move to a city that suited him better. One where they understood that tea meant iced, not hot—and *sweet,* for God's sake. Somewhere like Atlanta, New Orleans, or even Dallas. He could find plenty of easy marks in those cities, plenty of the stupid and greedy ready to lose their money to the clever and deserving.

He might not even have to leave here alone. Despite her lying, despite her betraying him to Ann, he was still attracted to Lauren. He'd always had a soft spot for redheads. And whatever money Lauren had left could help them get started. Shit, why not go legit? Set up a little business, something that would make his mama proud. What the hell, he could marry Lauren, have a passel of kids, be Mr. and Mrs. Respectable. Do a whole damned one-eighty with his life. He didn't have to let Ann call the shots. He had choices. This might be the biggest decision of his life. Time to re-evaluate his priorities.

• • • •

A half-hour later, James beat on Lauren's door. She wore only a towel clutched around herself when she opened the door, and she dropped that, backing away, as he barged in.

"Why the hell did you tell Ann about us?"

"Tell Ann?" She swept her hair behind her shoulders, fully revealing her nakedness. "Why would I do that?"

He hesitated. "You didn't threaten her?"

"Threaten her! With *what*?"

"Going to the police."

"What are you talking about, love?" Her thighs whispered, skin against skin, as she stepped closer. "Did Ann tell you that lie?"

James said nothing, but he clenched his jaw and looked away.

"Don't you see what she's doing, James? She feels threatened all right, but not from anything I said to her." Lauren's eyes glistened. "She's jealous of our love. She wants me out of the way."

"Yes," he said, looking her straight in the eye. "She does."

Lauren studied him, her face falling as she grasped his meaning. "I see." She swallowed hard. "So, you're here on Ann's orders?"

"I quote: 'One of us has to be removed from this cozy little triangle, James.'"

A single tear traced the curve of Lauren's cheekbone. "It doesn't have to be me."

"No," he said, "it doesn't."

Her lips slid into a tentative smile, and she reached out her arms to him. "Oh, love . . ."

He stepped back.

Slowly, she lowered her hands to her sides. Her smile remained.

"It doesn't have to be *only* you, Lauren." His tone was as black and sharp as an obsidian blade. "Truth is . . . I don't need either one of you. I deserve *all* the money I swindle."

Lauren gave no response, but James could have sworn her smile grew wider. He slipped his right hand into his jacket pocket. "Like you said, it was only a matter of time before Ann tired of me, and then where would I be? Gee, I don't know . . . best case scenario would be what . . . penniless in West Virginia with you?"

He paused, but still Lauren said nothing; she only looked past him with that weird smile—no, it had grown to a grin. Maybe she had flipped out on him. It didn't matter. He had just one more thing to say, and then he was done with her. "If there's one thing I know, *love*, it's that a con man must always stay one step ahead."

"And is that what you think you are, James?"

He whirled in time to see Ann raise her gun level with his heart.

"Ann, *wait*—"

"James, take your hand out of your pocket. That's a good boy. Now. Didn't you learn anything else from me? Didn't I teach you that you never *ever* run a con in your own backyard?"

"I don't . . . I wasn't—"

"Shut up, James. Preserve what little dignity you have."

He didn't dare let his eyes stray a millimeter from Ann, but he sensed that Lauren, though still behind him, had moved off to his right.

"Lauren, can you believe James has the balls to stand here and deny he's a self-serving, egotistical, ignorant son of a bitch?"

"Why, whatever do you mean?" Lauren said.

James could hear that goddam smile in Lauren's voice again. How long had she known his plans? "Ann, please, I made a mistake. I said some stupid things. But we're a good team. You need me."

"I *need* you?" Delicate hummingbird Ann now looked as warm and yielding as an ice sculpture. "Oh, James, James, James. Did you think this was my first pony ride? I do so love the benefits of my work, but I just hate to get my hands dirty. Lucky for me, I've always been able to attract an unlimited supply of 'brawn' like you. One beautiful man after another."

Fear and desperation hurled James back to his Alabama mountaintop Holiness roots. *Oh, Sweet Jesus, help me*! And just that quick, he knew he had a chance. He almost laughed with relief. Easy now. Be cool. "Heavenly father," he began, and as he sank to his knees, his right hand reached slyly downward, "forgive me for—"

Ann's bullet struck him dead center before his own gun cleared his pocket. The last voice he heard was Lauren's—"Nice work, Sis."

I never reckoned on moving to Kentucky. I was borned in West Virginia and figured to die there too. Just a flyspeck on the map, Iles Gap lies smack dab in the middle of coal country, and my daddy, like his daddy and granddaddy and great-granddaddy, worked the mines. He first went underground at sixteen, and by the time he died at forty-seven, his lungs was black and his skin blue. It weren't hard to see why he was dead set against any of his sons taking up that life, but wishing and getting is two different things.

At first, it seemed like he got his wish with my oldest brother. Soon as Levi could, he took off up North and found work in a Ford auto plant. But then he took to drink, lost that job, and landed back in Iles Gap, working in the coal dust. Tom might could have got hisself a college scholarship. I never knowed a body to read so many books. But at seventeen he done got his little gal in the family way and ended up down in the mine with Daddy and Levi.

I liked school and stayed in as long as I could, but by the time I was fourteen, Daddy was starting to fail. I scrabbled around taking whatever jobs I could find and taking over any chores Daddy had at home. But that weren't enough. When it became a struggle for Daddy to put in a full week in the mines, we all knew it was just a matter of time 'fore they cut him loose. With my brothers needing to support their own families, it fell to me to find a better way to help out Mama and Daddy. Hard labor didn't faze me none, but it would of killed me to be shut up somewheres inside, so I set my mind to farming.

Trouble was, there weren't much truck farming done in our part of West Virginia, and what farmers there was, had enough sons to do the work, so Mama wrote a letter to her cousin what lived in Kentucky to see could they use a hand. That's how come, when I was sixteen, I went to live two hundred miles from where I was borned.

After living in Kentucky less than a month, I got lonesome and homesick as all get out, but I never let on when I wrote to Mama. I knowed she sent me off for my own good. Mama's cousin couldn't take me in permanent, but she put the word out and got me hired on at a tobacco farm thereabouts. I never knowed the cousin anyways, so it didn't much matter to me.

It was the McNeery's first hired me. Owen and Maggie had ended up light on sons and heavy on daughters, and with planting about to commence, they needed a farmhand.

"Your Daddy farm, son?" Mr. McNeery asked.

"No, sir, he's a miner."

"You know anything about t'bacca?"

"Uh . . . well, sir, tell the truth, 'bout all I know is how to smoke it." Mr. McNeery snatched off his hat and scratched his head. I figured it was on his tongue to tell me I weren't the hand he was looking for, so I had to change his mind. "I'm a fast learner, sir, and I can do the work of two men."

He settled his hat back on his head and smiled. "One man's work will be sufficient, son. Let me show you where you'll bunk, and then we'll go on in to supper."

I sent Mama all but a few dollars of my wage every month. I weren't much on letter writing, but I always wrote a few words in answer to hers. Coming up on that first Christmas away from home, I feared I might spend the day bawling like a baby 'cause I missed it so, but when I opened Mama's December letter, out fell a bus ticket. I never was so glad to see a piece of paper in my life, but don't you know, when I showed it off at the supper table, the McNeery's daughter Carrie Sue went to crying. She weren't no baby, being one of the middle ones—about fifteen, I reckoned—and I never knowed why that ticket upset her till the day I left for home.

After I'd done climbed into the passenger seat of Mr. McNeery's pick-up truck, Carrie ran up to my window. "Merry Christmas, Jesse," she said and tossed a little package in my lap. The box looked right nice wrapped up in Christmas paper and a shiny bow. I turned my head to thank her, but she'd done run off. I took a peek at the tag and saw she'd signed it *Love, Carrie.* Right then and there that little Kentucky gal laid claim to a piece of my heart. I held back opening it, fearing what her daddy would think.

"Go ahead," Mr. McNeery said as we drove off toward the bus depot. "Let's see what she's up to."

It seemed a shame to ruin her handiwork, so I peeled back the paper, careful as I could. I lifted the lid of the little white box and fought back a blush and a frown at the same time. I weren't sure I wanted Mr. McNeery to see what she'd laid inside, but he craned his neck to get a look. It were a smooth river stone not much bigger than a quarter, but it weren't no ordinary stone. Only God knowed how many years of water flow had shaped it into a pert near perfect heart. Carrie'd slung it up in some braided black string, leaving the cord ends free and long. I didn't dare look at Mr. McNeery, but I felt his eyes weighing on me.

"What you fixing to do with that, son?"

"Sir?"

"My daughter's set her sights on you," he said. "You best think hard about it before you tie that around your neck."

"Yes, sir," I said, still not looking him in the eye. It'd be a lie if I said Carrie hadn't caught my attention. All the McNeery girls was easy on the eyes, but she had a special prettiness, like those girls in the movies, only she come by it natural. Her laugh sent a thrill right up my spine, and I confess I spent time out in the fields trying to think up clever things to say in her company, hoping to tickle her. Picturing her finding that stone and thinking of me sparked a battle between my spirit and my flesh. Praying Mr. McNeery weren't no seer, I shifted in my seat and pretended to look out my window.

That Christmas Eve, I knelt by the bed and said my prayers, and then I knotted them strings and hung that stone heart around my neck.

Carrie'd cut that cord at the perfect length. Her heart laid right next to mine.

• • • •

In all, I worked two years for Owen McNeery 'fore he became my father-in-law. Me and Carrie spoke our vows right after she come up seventeen. A week later, I took her home to Iles Gap to meet Mama and Daddy. Levi drove up from his house down river, and Tom and his wife lived right down the road, so Carrie got to meet my whole family. She charmed them all, even Tom.

The night 'fore me and Carrie left there, Tom called me outside for a smoke. We jawed some, and then he clapped me on the back. "You done good, little brother. Your Carrie's cute as a speckled pup." Them words coming from Tom, who always tried to outdo me at one thing or another, made my heart swell with pride.

Pride goeth before destruction and a haughty spirit before a fall. That's what the Bible tells, and I sure and certain proved that a truth. Owen and Maggie McNeery was good folk, and they welcomed me like a son, but I'd a mind to get my own place. A man ought to provide his wife with her own house to keep.

"It'll be heaven when we're on our own," Carrie said. "I just don't feel like a married woman waking up every morning in the same old bed I used to share with my sisters."

Yes, Carrie egged me on in my desire, but she was just young. I was young and *foolish*.

Owen and me was scything the path to the creek, a few days after I got back from home. "Now that I'm married," I told him, "Mama and Daddy won't take no more of my pay, so I'll be saving up quick as I can to get Carrie and me settled like a proper couple."

"That so," he said. We worked a spell 'fore he spoke again. "Me and Maggie started off in a place up near the head of that there creek. Little cabin, built by my granddaddy." He lifted his hat and wiped the sweat from his brow. "It's been home to nothing but snakes and critters for nigh onto twenty years." He turned in the general direction of the cabin and scratched his head slowly like he was studying on something. "You do the work to make it livable, son, and it's yours."

Soon as I told Carrie, she set about sewing curtains and whatnot. When she and her mama canned fruits and vegetables that summer, they put aside some jars of each to fill up Carrie's first pantry. I spent every spare moment up the creek clearing out and then fixing up that cabin from roof to floor. After the tobacco was hung to cure, I double-timed it and got the place ready 'fore Christmas.

I'd mowed down a good patch around the cabin and cleared a little garden space for Carrie to plant in the spring. We had us a solid roof over our heads, an ample wood pile, a clear well, a spring house, a root cellar, a chicken coop, and an outhouse. With our bedstead, a chifforobe and chest, a table and chairs, a cook stove, and a stocked pantry, we had us all the necessities, but I worried that Carrie would regret the loss of some of the conveniences she'd gotten used to at home.

"You're all I need to make me happy," she said.

In the dead of winter, there weren't much work to do for Owen, so Carrie and me spent a lot of time in our cabin. I did small jobs, fixing up things I hadn't got to 'fore we moved in. Carrie took to baking me cakes and pies. And sometimes she read to me while we cozied up in bed after making love. We for sure and certain had a good time at that part of marriage.

• • • •

"I love growing things," I said while we was planting peas in early March. Carrie got tickled at that.

"I'm growing something," she said, giggling.

"Well . . . sure . . . and when the soil warms up, you'll plant corn and beans and 'maters . . ." Oh, how her blue eyes lit up when she smiled like that. I grinned back.

She leaned in and knocked her little fist on my forehead. "How thick is that head of yours, Jesse Lee Aldridge?"

I stared at her a minute 'fore my mouth dropped open. *Numbskull.* "A baby?" She nodded. I pulled her to her feet and we danced a crazy little jig around that there garden. Weren't never a happier man in the world than me that day.

I worked like the devil that spring, doing my job with Owen and then running home to help Carrie get our own garden going. In no time, Carrie had it looking like a miniature version of her mama's and fussed over it so much I knowed she'd be a wonderful mama to our child. Half the mornings, after she'd done her own chores, she walked downcreek to visit with her mama and help out, but as her belly grew heavier, she took to staying up to the cabin more. Most days I'd run back to eat dinner with her. I had a mind to go on home that last day, but I'd caught my heel on a damn tree root and twisted my leg that morning, and by noontime my knee was swole up and throbbing something awful, so I decided to spare myself and just eat with the Mc-Neery's.

I knowed the Bible tells that God looks after the sparrows, but it also tells that all things work together for good, and what I never knowed is you have to suffer a heap of pain 'fore you learn that second lesson is the same as the first. When I limped home that last evening and found my Carrie, all I could do was rage at God. "She was just a sparrow! Why didn't you look after *her*?" Them was the last words I said to God for a long time.

The doctor told me about the afterbirth separating too soon. "Carrie was gone long before noon," he said, "and even if she'd been with her mama, it happened so fast we still might not have saved her."

"It ain't your fault, Jesse," said all her kin, crowded around me at the church. I didn't heed the words they spoke as they patted my shoulder or hugged me. My pretty little gal was dead. Her life'd drained out of her, leaving its trail in the dirt from the pole beans to the floor of our cabin. She died alone and scared. And I knowed she died calling my name 'cause I heard her voice in my nightmares. For a long time, I didn't want those nightmares to end. I deserved every one of them.

The McNeery's didn't hold me to blame, but I did. I bore the silences between me and Owen as we worked, and the pain in Maggie's eyes when she looked at me, but seeing Carrie's same blue eyes and blond curls on her sisters was the finger of guilt that poked and prodded me till I ran away. I fled back to West Virginia.

Once again, I found out there weren't nothing for me there. It were a life spent underground or nothing.

"Jesse Lee," Mama said, "you a-going down in those mines'll kill your Daddy faster than the black lung. You get along back to Kentucky now. Find you a job somewheres else iffen you can't bear a-seeing Carrie's folks, but you can't stay in this here godforsaken place."

I knowed Mama said that 'cause she loved me, and 'cause she saw how I walked out of the house, all tore up, every time Tom's wife came around, pregnant and packing another youngun on her hip. It was hard to stay, but harder to think about going. Daddy weren't long for this earth, and I knowed, if I left now, I'd never see him alive again.

He was too weak to do more than sleep most of the time, though most days he had me prop him up against some pillows so he could look out the window for a spell. Talking much brought on a coughing fit, so I would sit with him and tell him about growing tobacco. His eyes had that faraway look, and I'd tell myself he was picturing those fields in Kentucky, but in my heart I knowed he'd already sighted a land farther away than that.

One afternoon, when I told him I'd decided to stick around to help Mama and take care of him, the old fire sparked in his eyes. He raised a shaky hand to the steamed-up window. With his finger, he scrawled one word. *Go.*

Three months after I left, I came back here to Kentucky. I didn't know what the future held for me. I didn't have a place to live or work.

All I knew was that pain don't stay where it started. You can track across state and county lines, a river, and two mountains, but it'll dog your steps all the way. You best make your peace with it.

I lie in the dark and remember who I used to be. And who you were. And how we began.

You have no life, you said.

You were wrong. My life was simple, pared down. I drifted, free of entanglements. Free.

No one wants to be alone.

No one wants to be lonely. Lonely hurts. Alone was quiet, stable, manageable. Alone was simple.

You were made for me.

Like what. Like custom-made shoes? Like a made-to-order cake? I was whole. What part of me would you take for yourself?

Let me love you.

Let you fuck me. Love was complicated. Sex was simple. It had limited expectations, clear-cut scoring: cut and dried, do and done, good or bad. You demanded more.

Tell me your secrets.

So you could own me? I placed each stone in my wall precisely, just so. If I gave you one, the whole would fall.

You are everything I ever wanted.

Your need was greater than mine. You placed too great a burden on me. We were destined to fail, this couple you imagined us to be, this unified front against the world.

I want to spend my life with you.

I needed too much time alone. You took up all the space, all the air. You were a home invasion. I would not survive.

I have never been happier.

I had never been so scared. I could barely breathe. You complicated me.

You stir, in the dark, beside me. You murmur, moving closer, seeking me, even in your sleep. Your hand touches mine, clasps it in unconscious desire. You slipped under my skin, peeled it away, revealed me. Whole. Free.

I whisper into the dark, "I love you."

Sometimes, I think a sound disturbed my sleep the night of the Disappearance. Then other times, I wonder if it wasn't a sound but the silence. What I *know* is that everything in my life changed by the time I woke that next morning.

The first thing I noticed was the absence of the smell of Mom's every-Sunday-morning pancakes and bacon feast. On some level, I knew before I searched the house that my mom and dad and my brother, Josh, were gone. But gone had a different meaning back then. At first, I told myself I'd just forgotten that they'd planned to go somewhere without me, but I stopped pretending when I found both cars in the garage. That's when I got scared.

Texts wouldn't go through, so I dialed numbers like crazy—my parents, my friends, 9-1-1. Each time some stupid automated recording answered my call. My phone was still 65% charged when all the service bars disappeared. I went outside and tried calling 9-1-1 again but got nothing. That's when I freaked out.

I sat on our front steps hugging my knees and crying like a baby until panic sucked me dry and silenced me. We'd moved to Briarwood only two weeks before. I hadn't learned my way around the town yet. I didn't know anyone. I hadn't even met our neighbors. I didn't know where to go for help.

I'm only fourteen.

Trembling, I forced myself to walk to the front yard where I stood and yelled for my mom and dad until my throat ached. They didn't answer. No one answered. No one looked out a window. No one came out of the houses. That's when my brain sort of checked out. I sank to the grass, whimpering as I rocked back and forth.

Not long after, a woman jogged down the middle of our street. Being kind of out of it, I figured I was hallucinating, but I scrambled to my feet anyway. Then the full-on crazies took over, telling me the Disappearance might be her fault. I wanted to hide, but that message didn't reach my feet. I started screaming.

When she got closer, I saw the frantic look in her eyes and the index finger pressed to her lips. The gesture reminded me of my mom. I hushed. I'd never seen the woman before, but I wanted to hug her. I wanted her to hug me.

"It does no good to shriek," she said, slipping off her backpack and dropping to the grass. "You're the first person I've seen . . . or heard . . . since dawn."

I knelt beside her. "Where is everyone?"

"Gone."

．．．．

Gwen and I have been together for two days now. We walk because she says driving makes too much noise. She's more athletic than me. Runs marathons, she said and looks it with her thin body and short wash-and-wear hair. She's about my mom's age. That first day, I'd begged Gwen to stay with me at my house, but she refused.

"If I heard you screaming," she said, "it's likely someone else did too."

"But that's good, isn't it? Don't we want to find whoever's still here so together we can figure out where everyone else has gone?"

She shook her head. "Our first task is to get somewhere safe."

"Safe from what?"

Gwen didn't answer. I was too afraid to ask any more questions.

This morning, we found Miranda and Lucy within an hour of setting off. Without knowing it, they'd been wandering only six blocks apart. Miranda's about Gwen's age but more shapely. Like a lot of black women do, she wears her hair cropped close yet still looks feminine and beautiful. Lucy's younger. In her mid-twenties, I'd guess. She has long blond hair, like mine, but her skin's not so great.

Right now, Gwen is questioning them. Intensely. Like an interrogation. She pulled them aside making it obvious I'm not adult enough to hear what they're talking about. But whatever happened, happened to me too, so I don't know what they think they need to keep secret from me.

I didn't ask Gwen, but the way she expects everyone to follow her makes me think she's been in the military. So far, her main command is to be quiet. And her attitude makes it clear I'm not to question her decisions.

At the sound of tires squealing, the others stop talking. Gwen motions me over to the group. The three of them exchange looks while we sit in silence even though the car or truck or whatever it was is long gone. I can't stand feeling like I'm the only one that doesn't know what's going on.

"Shouldn't we go see—"

Gwen shakes her head at me, then stands and lifts her backpack into place. She starts off in the opposite direction the vehicle went. We fall in behind her. I assume we're going to walk as far away as possible from the squealing tires, but Gwen stops in front of a house in the middle of the next block. She motions for us to stay behind and then climbs the steps and tries the door. She enters. We wait. Maybe this will be our safe house.

After a few minutes, she comes back to the door and motions us to come in. It's safe, I guess. It smells terrible, though. There's spoiled food on the kitchen table. Miranda starts scooping it into a trash bag, and Lucy opens a few windows. No one speaks. That's hard for me, but I've almost gotten used to not talking much. What I haven't gotten used to is not having electricity and running water. No TV, no fridge, no showers—no toilet! But I don't hear them complaining, so I guess I'm being a baby about that stuff.

Gwen, who'd gone into the connected garage, comes back into the kitchen. "The people who lived here were campers. I've set up a chemical toilet out there. From now on, we'll travel at night. We're leaving here at first dark."

Miranda and Lucy nod. I want to ask why we can't stay in this house, but I don't. I wish someone would explain things to me.

Lucy finds an unopened jar of mayonnaise in the cupboard, so we mix some with cans of tuna and eat it with crackers. A cold soda would taste great right now, but I guess I'll get used to drinking it at room temperature. I wish I'd thought to bring along the chocolate chip cookies my mom baked on Saturday.

I wish I hadn't thought about my mom.

For most of the afternoon, Gwen sits on the floor of the living room by an open window. Sometimes she peeks out. A couple of times she makes the rounds of all the windows, but I think she's mostly listening. When the sun drops low in the west, she gives an order. "I saw at least two hiking backpacks in the garage; fill them with things we can use. Don't take the freeze-dried camper food; we can't use that until we ascertain the extent of our water supply. But get all the pantry food and bottled water we can carry."

Miranda, Lucy, and I sort through the cupboards, taking canned food, energy bars, and crackers. "If these people were campers," Lucy says, "they must have stuff like water purification tablets, which we'll need when we run out of bottled water." She heads back to the garage.

When we've packed as much as we can carry in our borrowed backpacks, we return to Gwen. I don't know what she heard or saw while we were out of the room, but now she says, "We'll stay here tonight."

Miranda and Lucy look like they want to question her, but Gwen shoots a glance at me and then stares them down. We each take an energy bar and a bottle of water for our dinner. When we're done eating, Gwen orders Lucy and Miranda to lay a mattress on the floor in the largest bedroom. I'm to sleep in the bed with Gwen, and the two of them will take the floor. We lie there in silence for a while, but none of us is sleeping.

"Do you think we'll find more people?" I ask.

"Shhh," Gwen whispers, but a few seconds later she says, "Probably not."

"But the four of us can't be all that's left."

"We're not," Miranda says, "and you know that as well as I do."

I'd heard traffic sounds a couple of times before today. And last night, I thought I heard screams in the distance, but I told myself I'd imagined that. "Why aren't we searching for those people?"

"Because we don't want to find them." Gwen rolls over, turning her back to me. "Go to sleep. We'll be setting off before dawn."

The thought that we were the only survivors in our town was horrible. The thought that we have to consider other survivors a threat is worse. I want this to be a nightmare. I can *wake* from a nightmare.

I'd swear I've just shut my eyes when Gwen shakes me awake.

"Everyone, grab your stuff," she says. "We're heading to the woods."

"In the dark?" Lucy sounds as alarmed as I am.

"We'll stick close to the edge. We need to find a place to set up base camp."

"But why in the—"

Gwen sighs. "*Not* in the woods, Lucy. Just farther out of town."

I head to the garage for one last use of the toilet.

* * * *

We're watching a house that sits highest on the hill above our town. We ended up here because all morning Gwen led the way just inside the tree line, gradually climbing. She stopped often, peering through her binoculars toward the town below. Every time one of us spoke to her, she shushed us. In late afternoon, we came to this large house at the edge of the woods. Gwen moved us farther back to a little rise among the trees and told us to rest. From this point, we can see the house but not be seen by anyone inside it.

In the last hour, all we've seen is a thin, gray-haired woman open the back door and walk to a shed in the yard. A few minutes later, she returned to the house. No one told me what we're supposed to be looking for, but the others haven't taken their eyes off the house, so I guess they know. I'm hungry and tired, and I want to go home.

A few minutes later, Miranda opens her pack and starts passing around dinner—cheese crackers and tomato juice. Lucy cuts an apple in quarters and shares. Living like a fugitive sucks. Up here where she doesn't have to worry about alerting anyone with the smell, I'll bet the woman in the house still cooks real meals.

I get sleepy after we eat. The third or fourth time I nod off and then rouse myself, I see Miranda leaning back against a tree, her eyes closed and mouth slack. Gwen's back is against another tree, her head resting on her knees.

Lucy smiles at me. "I'm keeping watch," she says. "Go ahead and nap."

She doesn't have to tell me twice. I curl up on the ground, hardly giving bugs a thought.

When I wake, it's already dark. A half-moon provides enough light for me to make out two silhouettes standing at the tree line. It's Miranda and Lucy, apparently still watching the house.

I move up beside them. "Where's Gwen?"

"Surveillance," Lucy says.

It's kind of funny how we're all picking up Gwen's jargon. "She's gone to the house?"

"Yes," Miranda says, "she's trying to determine if the woman is alone."

We watch in silence as clouds move in, blocking the moon's light. Gwen is only a few yards away before I realize she's walking toward us.

"Is she alone?" Miranda asks Gwen.

"I think so. I can't see the upstairs, of course, but she's sitting by herself reading . . . by candlelight."

I'm hoping Gwen thinks the woman is one of us, not one of the survivors we're hiding from. It's pretty chilly up here in the dark, and I'm spooked about spending the night in the woods.

"She just came out," Lucy whispers.

The woman is carrying a flashlight and moving toward the shed again. Miranda whispers what I'm thinking, "The shed must be her latrine."

Another Gwen word.

"I'm going back," Gwen says. "I'll be waiting when she comes out."

Seconds later, the clouds move away from the moon, and Gwen becomes visible, creeping toward the shed. When the woman opens the door, her flashlight illuminates them both. She jumps, startled, and at the same second Gwen grabs her and clamps a hand over the woman's mouth.

And that's how we meet Elizabeth, our fifth survivor. She welcomes us with tears of relief and a pantry full of food. Later, we strip and bathe in her pool under the inky sky. It feels great to go to sleep with a clean body and a full belly.

Though setting up base camp here seems like a good idea to me, I wake the next morning to an emotional discussion between Gwen and Elizabeth.

"But this is my *home*," Elizabeth says. "And I've been safe here. This location gives us an advantage. We can see most of the town from here. I've seen trucks driving around, and I hoped—"

"The advantage might not be to *us*," Gwen argues. "If we can see the whole town from up here, that means whoever's down there can see this house. And that means soon they'll realize this would be a great lookout for themselves."

Elizabeth says nothing, but tears shine in her eyes as her fingers caress the lid of the china sugar bowl sitting on the kitchen table. The patience and kindness in Gwen's voice when she continues surprises me.

"We need to be as invisible as possible, Elizabeth. The worst thing we can do is call attention to ourselves."

From my experience, it's useless to argue with Gwen, but Elizabeth doesn't know that. I go to the living room where I can see the town from a window. How many trucks has Elizabeth seen? Evidently, from the way Gwen cut her off, whoever's in those trucks are the people we don't want to find. The others still don't talk about them in front of me, but like Miranda said, I'm not stupid. The truck people are dangerous.

In the end, Elizabeth wins out. Gwen decides the advantages of the house location outweigh the risks. She assigns us tasks to minimize some of those risks. Lucy and Miranda dig a proper latrine on the west side of the house, the one not facing the town or woods, and they rig up a tarp shelter around it. Gwen and Elizabeth clear the master bedroom and pull in enough mattresses for us all. It's safer if we stick together as much as possible.

I make sure all the windows have adequate covering. All blinds or curtains on the front windows will stay closed and drawn at all times because they are the most visible from town. Gwen is thrilled to discover that Elizabeth has a telescope, which she sets up in front of an attic vent, focused on the town. She says we'll take turns on watch.

Sometimes I feel like this is all a weird adventure, and then wham! Reality hits, and I feel like I'm going crazy. Maybe I'm *already* crazy. How could any of this really be happening? Tomorrow will be Saturday. But just *last* Saturday afternoon, I went to the mall with Alyssa and Chloe. Last Saturday night, we went to a party, and Kyle and I spent the whole time together in the upstairs hall. Next month, I'm going to be fifteen. Mom's planned a big party for me. My real life couldn't have ended on Sunday. It just couldn't.

• • • •

We've been at Elizabeth's for two weeks. Gwen and Miranda and even Lucy tried to keep the seriousness of our situation from me as much as they could. But now they can't hide anything because Lucy hurt her back digging the latrine and can't carry much weight, and Elizabeth is old and would slow us down, so it's up to Miranda, Gwen, and me to scavenge. There's still food in Elizabeth's pantry, but we need water, water, water. And Lucy says we need more protein sources since we no longer have meat. Just our luck that Elizabeth's stove is electric—no hot meals for us. So we have to scavenge for supplies we need. It's not hard, but it's scary because we have to do it in the daylight.

"Be chameleons," Gwen says.

I barely breathe the whole time we're out.

When Gwen told me not everyone who survived was like us. I didn't really understand what she meant. I do now. We've watched them through the telescope. As far as we can tell, there's one group of seven or eight men, like a pack of wolves on wheels. Marauders, Elizabeth called them. They don't try to be quiet like we do.

"Intimidation," Gwen says. "They want us to know they're out there. They want us to know they're on the hunt."

"Are you saying they know about us?" Elizabeth asks.

Gwen doesn't get time to answer before Lucy butts in, "They don't know we're up here though, right?"

"If I thought that, Lucy, we wouldn't still be here, but we have to assume they're aware there might be survivors they haven't found yet. That's why they hunt."

On previous scavenging trips, we've found some of their prey—the survivors they found. An old man, naked and beaten so badly he looked like a bloody lump of dough, they'd left on a lawn strewn with empty liquor bottles. Brutality and murder had been their party entertainment. At another house, they'd dropped a cement block into a pool. Tied to it was a little boy, maybe only six years old. I threw up when we found him.

But the ones that *scared* me, the ones I can't quit thinking about, are the three women we found. Naked. Savaged, is how Miranda describes them. Raped is what she means. Raped, torn, bitten, mutilated—savaged, yes.

I was in shock those first days after the Disappearance. I followed Gwen around like some robot. Now that I've seen and heard the Marauders, the full reality of our situation has seeped in, but I try not to think about it one second more than necessary.

Once the five of us established that we were all clueless about what happened between midnight and dawn on the first Sunday in June, we made a pact to block our thoughts of life before the disappearance. "No BD," the others say quickly when one of us slips and wishes for something in the past or mentions one of the missing. We *have* to do that. It's the only way to keep from totally freaking out.

But what the Marauders did to those women was not *BD*. It's now. It's what they do when they discover a woman in hiding. I've prayed a million times they never find us.

As much as possible during the day, we stay out of sight, always alert for sounds of the Marauders' trucks. We can hear them coming from a long distance because the quiet hides nothing. One day, they found someone hiding not too far from where we were gathering supplies. We heard the screaming. I hid my face, trembling until it stopped.

It's amazing how few sounds there are now. The birds came back to the woods last week. I like to close my eyes and listen to them. For those few moments, I'm not scared. I almost feel normal.

• • • •

This morning, Elizabeth suddenly remembered she had an old battery-operated radio in a closet—she's kind of senile, I think. Miranda picked up a weak signal on it, but even though we couldn't make out any words, it sounded like more than just static. Even Gwen got excited. Miranda says the batteries we found in one of the kitchen drawers had probably lost their strength, so on our next scavenging trip, we'll get more. I can't wait.

Lucy and I are on laundry duty today. That's a joke. We can't spare any water to wash clothes. What we do is make a list of what items we're almost out of: clean underwear, of course; shirts; jeans; and whatever else we need to get on our next *shopping trip*, which is what Lucy calls our supply runs. I think even Elizabeth has about gone through all her clean clothes. We've had to slack off on personal hygiene lately. At first, we all used the swimming pool to bathe and wash our hair, but now it's all mucked up without the filter running. I don't want to think what it's going to smell like in another month when the weather's hotter. Oh crap, what will *we* smell like? Dry shampoo and baby wipes can only do so much.

"Do you think we'll pick up a signal on that radio?" Lucy asks me.

"I hope so, but don't you think it's weird that Gwen didn't think about finding an old radio long ago? And why hasn't she looked for guns? Being ex-military and all."

"Where'd you get the idea she's military?"

"I . . . well, I just assumed it from the way she took charge."

"She told me she's a scout leader."

"Oh."

I wish Lucy hadn't shared that bit of info. If Gwen only knows about camping and stuff, how's that going to help us with the Marauders?

"Can you shoot a gun?" Lucy asks.

"No.

"Me either," she says. "Miranda's a lawyer, by the way."

I like that Lucy speaks in present tense, like Miranda is *still* a lawyer. It gives me hope we're going to be all right. Everyone who's missing will return, and life will get back to normal.

"What are you?" I ask.

"Me?" She laughs. "I'm a dietitian. Real handy right now, huh?"

• • • •

The radio sounds get louder when we put in the new batteries, but that's all. As soon as it's dark, Miranda and Gwen take it outside. Right now, they're walking around trying to find a stronger signal. Me and Elizabeth and Lucy are sitting silently around the kitchen table like we might pick up the signal too if we're quiet. When the back door opens, we all suck in air so fast and hard, I'm surprised the room didn't implode or something.

It takes only a few seconds to walk from the door into the kitchen, but it seems like forever before Miranda says, "We heard something."

There's a tiny tea light on the table. That's as much light as we dare on moonless nights, but it's enough to see that Miranda's eyes are shining. She takes a breath and Gwen jumps into the pause.

"It's weak and breaks up, but we're sure we heard the words *come* and *Ohio*."

"It sounds like a repeating message," Miranda adds.

"A recorded one?" Elizabeth asks.

Disappointment is obvious in her voice, or maybe it's just because the same thought occurred to me. It could be just some emergency broadcasting thing.

"I don't think so," Miranda says. "There's variation in tone. It sounds live."

"We're going back out," Gwen says. "We just came in to let you know we could stay outside until near dawn, so you might as well go on to bed."

Gwen grabs granola bars, while Miranda fills empty bottles with the cold-brewed coffee Lucy makes. They'll be on sound surveillance, I guess.

As Gwen and Miranda head back outside, Elizabeth picks up the candle, and the three of us go upstairs. We lay in the dark, silent, but I don't think any of us will sleep much. I think we're all wondering how we can get to Ohio. We can't walk all that way, but maybe if we can sneak out of town, we'll find a car with a full tank and we'll drive until it's out of gas, and then we'll find another one, and then . . . well, we'll use however many cars it takes us to get to Ohio.

If there's a will, there's a way, my dad always says. For sure, we have the will.

. . . .

Gwen and Miranda have nothing new to report in the morning. They picked up snatches of the same message, but we know nothing more about what's in Ohio than we did last night. I'm sitting on the living room floor watching Gwen, Miranda, and Elizabeth play some old card game like they're on automatic pilot. Lucy is reading a romance novel—or pretending to. No one speaks. I don't know why. Shouldn't we be trying to come up with a plan to get to Ohio?

It's hot and stuffy in here today. This house will feel like a sauna by next month. The longer we wait to start traveling, the worse it will be. I get up and walk to the back of the house to sit below the one window that's open a few inches. No breeze. If only I could walk across the backyard and into the shady woods, where it's cool and the air is fresh. Sometimes, I feel so trapped. I'm afraid I'll freak and run out the front door screaming.

The Marauders have imprisoned us. And today we're even more stressed than usual because we don't know what they're up to. We haven't heard or seen any trucks or motorcycles for at least thirty-six hours. Hours. Hours mean nothing and everything now. Sixty minutes more of this insanity. Sixty minutes closer to . . . what? Escape? Freedom? Or—I can barely stand to think it—death?

. . . .

Two mornings later, Elizabeth wakes us before dawn. "The trap door," she says.

"What?" Lucy mumbles.

"She's talking in her sleep," Miranda says and rolls over.

"No. It's real," Elizabeth says. "I forgot all about it."

Gwen sighs. "Are you talking about the basement?"

"No, this isn't connected to the *basement*." Elizabeth is touchy about having the state of her memory pointed out. "It's a secret hideaway. A crawl space. My husband believ—"

"Where's this trap door?" Gwen is up and pulling on her jeans.

"In the living room."

We're all up now and following Gwen down the stairs.

Elizabeth directs Gwen to move the sofa and pull back the corner of the area rug. Gwen does that and then lifts the door. Miranda, who has a flashlight in hand, drops down into the crawl space. Silently, we watch the light grow dimmer as Miranda moves farther away from the opening. A minute later she's back and hoisting herself out.

"Nothing down there except an ancient survival kit."

We all laugh. I don't know why.

"How big is the crawl space?" Gwen asks. "Could we all fit down there? If we needed to."

Miranda nods.

"But if we *all* go down, they'll see the trap door." Miranda doesn't need to define who *they* are.

"Only if they lift up the rug," Lucy says.

Miranda shakes her head. "We can't pull the rug back over it after we're down there, Lucy."

"We could try attaching the rug to the door," Gwen says, "but it would be better if we disguised it another way." She studies the room for a moment. "If we rearranged the room to sit the rocking chair over it, that wouldn't look odd, and—"

"We could attach the chair *and* the rug to the door," Lucy says, catching Gwen's train of thought. "That way the chair would tilt over when we opened it but sit back upright when we closed the door behind us."

"Hot damn, I think you've got something," Miranda says.

I don't understand why they're excited about this. "But we don't need a hiding place. Aren't we leaving for Ohio?"

They all look at me, but none of them answers.

· · · ·

With everyone working on rigging up the chair over the hiding place, we got a little lax with surveillance, which was really stupid. While we were preoccupied, the Marauders moved into a house on the street below us. The smell of their barbecue alerts us just seconds before Lucy, her face chalky, runs inside from the latrine.

"They're here," she whispers and then collapses on the kitchen floor.

"Nobody make a sound," Gwen hisses.

From the looks of us, all sitting or kneeling on the floor around Lucy, making a sound is the last thing on anyone's mind. Do they already know we're here? What if they'd seen one of us move past a window? How far do our normal voices travel through the silence surrounding us? Oh, God. They're barbecuing. What if they've been hunting in the woods behind this house?

An hour inches by. In silence, we pass around a bottle of water Miranda reached up to grab off the counter. A couple of hours later, when Elizabeth signals that her bladder simply won't hold any longer, Miranda points her to the planter in the corner that held a fern until it dried up.

The Marauders have reduced us to animals.

We huddle until we hear their trucks roar down the street at sunset, but even then, we only whisper and crawl through the downstairs rooms. We eat very little for supper, and though no one says it, I figure we're all wondering the same thing. How long before we dare sneak out to scavenge more supplies?

The best I manage for most of the night are snatches of semi-sleep, the kind where you can't really tell if you dozed off or just think you did. The tossing and sighing around me signals the others are in the same state, but just before dawn, I slip into a dream about my boyfriend, Kyle. We're kissing, which is as far as I ever let him go, and then he pulls me closer and closer until I realize he won't stop, he's going to crush me to death. Gwen shakes me awake to hush my whimpering.

For the next two days, the Marauders torture us with their presence.

Elizabeth cries most of our waking hours. Miranda threatens to strangle her if she doesn't stop, and Lucy threatens to beat the hell out of Miranda if she doesn't quit yelling at Elizabeth. Actually, no one yells. We're all so terrified we barely whisper.

Gwen says little to any of us. She just stares at nothing. I keep thinking about my dream and then the very real nightmare of the women the Marauders have killed.

Every second, I hate them more for turning us into animals like them. A five-gallon bucket Gwen brought in from the garage and put in the basement is our new latrine. I can't let myself think what will happen when we fill that up. They corralled us when we were already low on supplies, and we haven't dared to leave the house since.

On the third day, Lucy hands out bottles of water. "Make it last. There's no more."

"I read once," Miranda says in the dark bedroom that night, "that you have a better chance of surviving if you humanize yourself to your attacker. Force them to see you as a *person*."

"Oh, God," croaks Elizabeth and starts crying again.

No one tells her to shut up.

• • • •

We wake to engines gunning. The Marauders are closer. Elizabeth's house sets back from the street on a rise. By the time we dress and go downstairs, they're roaring down the street just fifty yards below the house. We don't look out the windows. We don't even look at each other. We just sit in silence on the kitchen floor, as far away from them as we can get.

An hour or so later, after they tire of their game and leave, Gwen goes into the pantry and brings us canned beans and fruit to eat.

"We have to keep up our strength," she says.

Miranda starts laughing. She laughs until her face is wet with tears. She doesn't stop until Elizabeth slaps her across the face. Then they cling to each other. Lucy sits against the wall, eyes closed and lips moving soundlessly.

"I'm sorry," Gwen says. "I thought we could hide until . . . I thought they'd leave town. I should have . . . I let you all down. I'm so sorry." She hides her face and sobs.

I feel sick.

Gwen is the strong one. Our leader. If she's breaking down, what hope is there for the rest of us? Did those other women, those dead women, have hope? When the Marauders came for them, did they mistake them for rescuers at first?

I crawl into the room Elizabeth calls the den and head straight for the desk. It takes only seconds to find what I'm looking for. No one followed me, so I do what I have to do right there. It's my only chance. I can't end up like those savaged women. I'm only fourteen. I'm a virgin. I'm a good girl.

Why didn't I disappear with my mommy and daddy and my little brother?

• • • •

The Marauders start up again in the afternoon. Now they're not only driving up and down the street, they stop in front of our house and yell to us. They're calling us nasty names and telling us to come out and play.

Gwen filled two empty water bottles with juice, one from cans of pineapple and the other from cans of tomatoes, and she and Miranda put the juice, some food, blankets and pillows, and another bucket into the crawl space. She left the trap door up. Now we're all sitting on the living room floor staring at it.

I can't let myself believe we're actually going to hide down there. I can't let myself believe any of this is real. This has to be a nightmare. It just *has* to be. Whole towns of people don't just disappear. That's impossible. Any minute now, I'm going to wake up in my own bed. It will be Sunday. Mom will be making pancakes. And dad will knock on my bedroom door and call me sleepyhead. And Josh will try to grab all the bacon. I'll wake up. I will. I *have* to.

I wake from my daydream when Gwen gives me a push toward the trap door. When I hesitate, she grabs my wrists and pulls me across the floor.

"Down," she orders. I drop down and she follows, pulling the door closed over us. The others are already there. Elizabeth is pale and her eyes are closed. Miranda's and Lucy's faces are shiny with tears. They pull me close and hug me. Then they push me behind them.

"Scoot as far back as you can," Lucy whispers.

"Hide in the darkest corner," Miranda adds.

As I do what they told me, the first footsteps sound on the floorboards above us. Before Gwen turns off the LED lantern, I see she's holding a knife, the kind hunters use. Miranda picks up a baseball bat and Lucy a fireplace poker. They're ready to fight.

Then we're sitting in total darkness listening to the Marauders search the house. They call out to each other, some upstairs, some downstairs. Then for a few minutes, it's quiet. Have they gone so soon?

A loud crash above us nearly frightens a scream out of me. My heart pounds so hard I'm sure they'll hear it through the floorboards. One of the Marauders lets out a laugh that sounds insane.

"It's cocktail time, cunts," one of them yells. "Come out, come out, wherever you are."

More laughter. More voices join in. Oh, God. They must be right above us, in the living room. I can't take this. I'm going to scream. I'm going to get us all killed. I clamp my hands over my mouth. And even though I can't see a thing anyway, I squeeze my eyes closed. I try to breathe slower, deeper. I can't be a baby. I can't—

Everything explodes.

My eyes fly open just in time to see Gwen jerked upward through the trap door opening. Her knife falls, stabbing only the dirt floor.

A filthy brute drops into the crawl space, leering at Miranda and Lucy. "Hello, ladies."

Miranda lunges at him, but a second man has dropped into our hideout, and he kicks her in the stomach. Lucy screams as the first man grabs her by the hair and drags her to the opening. Hands reach down and pull her up and out of sight. The second man, who'd been steadily kicking and punching Miranda, lifts her to the trap door, and she disappears too.

The first man crawls over to Elizabeth. Her eyes are still closed. He backhands her and she falls sideways without a sound. "The old bag's dead," he calls out.

Elizabeth's lucky. But maybe I'm lucky too because he doesn't glance back to where I am. The light spilling down from the living room doesn't reach where I'm crouched. He climbs back out of the crawl space.

But he doesn't close the trap door. Even though I jam my fingers as far into my ears as they'll go, I hear everything. After a while, I lean over and vomit till I'm empty.

Finally, the thumps and screams and sickening cheers stop. The Marauder's voices drift away. I stifle another scream when truck engines roar to life. They're leaving. They don't know I'm here.

I listen for a while longer before I move. On my hands and knees, I creep forward until I'm under the trap door opening. With Gwen's knife in my hand, I rise just enough to see into the living room. The front door stands open. No one's in sight. I reach up, preparing to hoist myself into the room. My left hand lands in something sticky. Something red. I gag, but I have nothing left to vomit.

Crouching on the living room floor beside the upturned chair, I discover I was wrong. The room isn't empty. But it's perfectly still. Two bloody feet and calves extend into the room from the hall. I want to pretend I don't know whose they are, but the skin color gives it away. And a glance to my right reveals tangled blond hair hanging over the arm of the sofa. I don't see Gwen's body, but my heart tells me it's here somewhere.

Please, God, help me. I'm the only one left alive. And I don't know what to do.

"Well, lookee here."

Terror launches me to my feet and turns me to face the black-eyed monster standing in the front doorway. With more instinct than aim, I fling the knife at him.

"You fucking *bitch,*" he screams when it hits him.

I don't know where the knife stabbed him because I'm already sprinting toward the back door. If I can make it to the woods, maybe I have a chance. Maybe I can run all the way to Ohio.

I'm halfway across the backyard when he tackles me.

He rolls me onto my back. Blood soaks the shoulder of his shirt, but the wound isn't slowing him down. He slices open my shirt with the knife. Surprised, he pauses for a moment. He's looking down at me, reading what I've written on my stomach. He laughs. That insane laugh.

"So, Amy Walls, is it? Nice to meet ya, sweetcakes. But you ain't gonna say the same about me." He jerks down my shorts.

"Please, don't. Please, stop." Oh, God. It hurts so much. I want to see the sky, but he's on top of me, blocking it out, crushing me. Pain. It's all I feel. Please. Stop.

I quit struggling.

I drift.

I drift away.
I'm so cold.
I can't see.
Help me. Somebody.
Please, Daddy, help me.
Please, God.

. . . .

Oh.
Look.
The sky is so blue.
Someone golden lifts me.
Who are you?
A friend.
Do I know you?
Yes.
Your eyes . . . silver light.
I'm here to save you.
Save me?
I'll take you to Ohio.
Is my family there?
Yes. All are there.

"Y'all ain't nothin' but ignorant trash," I yell at the passing carload of boys. Look at 'em, hanging out the windows, cat-calling and making lewd gestures with their beer bottles. Ain't that just proving me right? I turn my head and keep on walking toward Pike's Drugs. There's a world of difference between me and their kind. I have ambition. And that's what'll get me out of this town.

I ain't gonna end up like my momma. No passel of kids and a body worked to the bone for me. I'm too smart for that. Everybody tells me so. Two more years up at the high school, and then Mossy Creek's gonna see my heels kicking up dust. I'm headed up to Greenville where I can go to community college.

"Aw, don't talk like that, Kelly Jean," Lonnie Jr. tells me. "Me and you's made for each other." After he graduates next month, he'll go to work in the paper mill, like his daddy and brothers. "I'll make plenty of money," he says. "Enough to support a wife, that's for sure." He has plans. He's gonna save up for a down payment on a house. Except sometimes, he says, "Maybe I'll get me a brand new truck first. We can always live with my momma or yours for a spell after we get married."

"There ain't enough money in the world to make me marry you," I tell him, but he don't listen. He's too busy climbing on top of me.

I'm on to his tricks. He knows, without permission from my momma and daddy, I can't get birth control pills until I'm sixteen, yet he keeps "forgetting" to pack condoms. That's why I'm the one walking into this drug store right now. I ain't letting his plans mess up mine.

What I'm here for is on the back wall next to the pharmacy counter, so I stop in the makeup aisle and poke around at a lip-gloss display. I can't just march back there and grab a pack. I need to make sure no busybody spots me. Mr. Bradley don't worry me none. A pharmacist is kind of like a doctor or a priest or something. He won't tell.

"Hey, Kelly Jean."

I look up towards the front checkout. Oh, shit. It's my momma's second cousin Ruth. "Hey, Ruth," I say. "Just killing some time." You might think she'd be happy to know I'm smarter than my momma, but no, she'd go flapping her jaw. Like me buying a few "rubbers" is the biggest scandal in *this* town.

A customer steps up to Ruth's cash register, so I take that opportunity to head toward the pharmacy. I stop on the way to grab an issue of *People* and a pack of Skittles so it won't look I came in to buy just the condoms. Before I get to the end of the aisle, I spy someone picking up a prescription. After a pause, I inch forward until I make out who it is. Well, ain't I the lucky one. It's only Mr. Honeycutt. He's pretty new in town. He don't know me by sight, and he don't really know my kin. Wait. *Dammit to hell.* Mr. Anderson just walked up behind him. Running into my English teacher at a time like this ain't lucky after all.

I duck into the "feminine needs" aisle to wait until they leave. No man's gonna pay much attention to a girl trying to decide which tampons to buy. Speaking of which, I might as well get some. My period's due in . . .

Oh, Jesus.

Near midnight, Stan entered his silent house through the back door. He didn't bother to turn on the kitchen light before grabbing a beer from the fridge and continuing on to the living room. It wasn't much brighter there, lit only by the green-shaded desk lamp. He opened the bottle, tossing the cap in the general direction of a wastebasket in the corner, and dropped into his recliner positioned in front of the TV. For once, he didn't pick up the remote. He stared at the empty spaghetti sauce jar sitting on the desk across the room. Well, not exactly empty.

As he stared, he drank. And as he drank, he twisted the hair just behind his right ear. He had half a mind to go back down to Jack's Tavern with that jar. That's what he should have done in the first place. He'd love to see their faces when they got a look inside. He'd say, "Yeah. Uh-huh. Whaddya say now, jerkoffs?"

Hell, maybe tomorrow he'd take that thing over to the taxidermist across the river. Then he'd hang it from his truck's rearview mirror. Stan huffed a laugh. "Yeah, just as macho as hanging a ten-pound largemouth on your wall, right?" He took the last swig of beer, sat the bottle on the floor, and launched himself out of the chair.

He picked up the jar and sighed. The only way he could prove he wasn't lying was to show the guys at Jack's what he held in his hand, but that's the very thing he couldn't do. There were laws against what he'd done, though exactly how those laws applied in this case, he couldn't be sure. And he damned well couldn't ask the cops.

"You're loony," they'd say. "The drink's gone to your brain," they'd say. "Just like your old man."

True he'd put away a beer or thousand in his thirty-nine years, but he wasn't crazy. He had the proof. Evidence, if you wanted to look at it that way. But for how long? Even though he'd poured—shit, *wasted*—a whole pint of vodka in this jar, the damned thing had already started to change. It would rot. How the hell was he supposed to know how to preserve something like this?

Stan put down the jar and went back to the kitchen. He stood looking out the window as he tipped up another beer. The guys had pissed him off tonight. Humiliated him. Hell, it wasn't like he'd climbed on the bar and shouted his story to strangers in the bar. Only his three closest friends, his buddies, his pals had sat around the table in the back corner. Only the three guys he thought he could trust. And they'd laughed at him. Took it as a joke.

"That's a good one," Dave had said, slapping him on the back.

"Bring this comedian another cold one on us," Pete called out to Rosie. "Hey, here's Joey. Pull up a chair. Stan's got a story for ya."

Stan started over from the beginning. Maybe if he added more detail this time, they'd believe him. "I was walking home last night, taking the shortcut through that vacant lot on Branford, ya know? The heat these last two weeks dried up all those weeds, so at first I thought what I saw was just seeds—those fluffy kind, ya know? I thought it was seeds flying around 'cause I was disturbing them weeds, cutting through the field like that. But then I heard the hum. Like a swarm of bees . . . those big black and yellow ones—"

"Bumblebees," Joey offered.

"Yeah, like bumblebees. But every time I tried to see one, like get one in focus, they disappeared or something."

"Wait," Joey said, "were you coming from here?" He gestured tipping up a beer to his mouth.

"Yeah, I was coming from here, but I wasn't drunk. Dave'll tell ya." Stan waited for Dave to nod confirmation to Joey. "So something was buzzing and flitting all around me, and it finally occurred to me it was grasshoppers, and that's why I couldn't actually see 'em. Remember how hard it was to catch the suckers when we was kids? Ya'd spot 'em and grab quick, but the things jumped so fast it was like they just disappeared."

Stan took a long pull at his beer. "So, I stopped walking. Stood still as a post. And then I heard another sound above the buzz. Like ... well, like nothing I ever heard before except maybe in a movie. Yeah, like one of those kiddie movies or cartoons where they have little mice or something chattering in tiny, high-pitched voices, ya know?" He shut up for a minute, trying to remember if he'd heard any actual words.

"It was mice?" Joey asked. "Flying around?" He laughed. "And you's say ya wasn't drunk."

"I *wasn't* drunk ... not when I left here and for damned sure not when I saw what it really was." Around the table, Dave and Pete leaned in as if they hadn't already heard the story. Maybe they thought he'd slip up, and then they'd hoot and holler, telling him to keep his lies straight. But the truth is the truth.

"When I stood still, they drew closer. Hovered, like. I couldn't see 'em in detail, but I was about halfway between the streetlights on Branford and the ones on Sixth, so I could see good enough." Stan took another drink, for dramatic effect sort of, and glanced at Dave and Pete before he set his glass down. He wiped the back of his hand across his mouth and turned to Joey. "They was fairies."

Joey looked him in the eye, and then glanced at the other guys. A grin twitched at the corners of his mouth, but he waited for the punch line.

Stan held up a hand, palm out. "Swear to God."

"Fuck you," Joey said and laughed. Dave and Pete laughed with him. And the hotter Stan's face grew, the harder they laughed.

· · · ·

That's when he'd shoved away from the table and walked out without another word. There was more to the story than he'd told them, but he didn't have the guts to tell it. How the fairies—seven or eight of them—had clustered together no more than three feet from his face. How he'd heard them talking to each other in those reedy little voices that set his nerves on edge, partly from the sound and partly because he couldn't make out the words. It occurred to him, now, that they might have spoken their own language.

Stan had been too embarrassed to tell the guys the whole story. But really, could you blame a man for freaking out? What was he supposed to do? He'd been walking along, minding his own business, just trying to get home to his bed. He was a stand-up guy. A hard worker. Took care of his old ma and his retar—*mentally disabled*—kid brother. Even plopped down in a pew at St. Joseph's on occasion. Christmas and Easter, at least. He was a stand-up guy.

He just didn't have any experience with running into fairies in a vacant lot in the neighborhood where he'd lived his whole life. And those freaky little things had started it. *Damn them.* Riling him up with the way they stared at him, talking about him, and then whirring around his head again. What man wouldn't have defended himself? Why, it was just a natural reaction to swat at something like that. Wasn't it? Even if the swat *was* more like a swing.

How could he have known how fragile the things were?

Stan left the half-emptied beer bottle on the kitchen table and returned to the living room. He pulled out the desk chair and dropped into it with a sigh. He hadn't really meant to keep her as a trophy. True, on the way home last night, he'd thought about the bird cage in his garage, but he hadn't really intended to put her into it. He wasn't serious about the taxidermy thing either.

You had to give him credit for picking up the fairy, gently, instead of running away. Well, truth be told, he did run but only because he had the cockamamie idea he could help her if he got her back here quick enough. Then one look at the odd angle of her head and the way it lolled as he lifted her limp body from his hand to the bathroom counter collapsed all hope of that.

Saving her was the only reason he'd brought her here. If she'd lived, he was sure he would have let her fly away. Pretty sure.

Now, here he sat, alone with a dead fairy floating in a jar of vodka glowing sickly from the green lamp light. Why hadn't he thought to close her eyes? They were large in her tiny face, the sky blue gone milky now. Her blond hair was pulled up and knotted on top of her head. Damned if Disney hadn't got it almost right. No bright green tunic, though. She wore a kind of mottled tan and olive body stocking. Camouflage. Her wings, larger than the cartoon kind, looked like veined cellophane. The upper third of one had crumpled—from her fall or his backhanding, he didn't know.

Either way, it was his fault, wasn't it?

He studied her for a long time. It was her tiny fingers and toes, complete with pink nail polish, that did him in. It was that human resemblance that crushed him, shamed him, made the tears track down his cheeks and into the stubble along his jaw. He rubbed his face dry, angry, disgusted with himself. How could he have kept her in a jar? Somebody loved her. Missed her. Was she a daughter, a sister, a wife? Oh dear God, was she a mother?

He hid his face behind murderous hands. His stomach churned. Why had he told the guys? They hadn't believe him—*said* they hadn't. But what if they got curious? What if they went to the lot searching for the other fairies? What if his sorry attempt to impress his friends with a big story of his own for once, ended in a blood bath?

Stan grabbed the jar. In the bathroom, he opened it and plunged his fingers into the vodka. Tenderly, he grasped one of her arms and lifted her out onto a towel. He patted her dry and, finally, closed her eyes. Then he went to his bedroom in search of something suitable to wrap her in. He tore apart his bureau drawer until he remembered the silk handkerchief in the breast pocket of his good black suit. His funeral suit. As he arranged her on the white square, he wondered what her name was. Something pretty, he imagined.

With the tiny, shrouded figure cupped in one hand, he headed toward Branford Avenue. He'd just rounded the corner and started down the last block when he stopped cold. What the hell would he do if the guys were at the lot? Even if they'd seen nothing there, they'd see what he carried. Stan slipped his hand into his jacket pocket and left the silken bundle there. If he played it just right . . . "Yeah, ya saw right through me, guys. I should have known I couldn't fool ya. Nothing exciting ever happens to Stan, right?"

He'd do whatever he had to do or say, whatever it took to get the guys to leave, because he had to get the fairies to show themselves to him again. He had to make things right.

He worried for nothing. The field was empty—or maybe not. He walked farther in and stopped to listen. He lifted the fairy from his pocket and held her out, cradled in both hands. "I'm sorry," he whispered. A distant hum was the only response. "I didn't mean to hurt her."

The hum grew louder. Suddenly, shadowy figures zipped and darted around him. A wing clipped his ear.

"I brought her back to you," he said. The silk brushed across his fingertips and then she was gone, carried away in a flurry of wings.

The hum grew to a furious buzz as a single line of fairies hovered in front of him. Stan almost smiled at the sight of these small, but obviously male, muscular bodies dressed in black like a fantastical, miniature SWAT team. He couldn't make out their expressions, but no doubt they were serious. This was no time for levity.

"I'm sorry," he said again, setting off a furious high-pitched response he couldn't decipher. The actual words didn't matter; he understood their intent. They'd judged him guilty. And he was. He wouldn't deny it. His cowardice had cost a life. *Man up, Stan.*

The warriors realigned themselves, splitting into pairs, each fairy holding one end of a coiled black wire.

They were more serious than he'd thought. Oh, God. Trembling, Stan held up his hands. "Wait," he said. "Wait. I didn't know . . . I didn't think . . . I didn't mean to . . ."

At lightning speed, each fairy team stretched their wire taut and flew around his neck in opposite directions.

He never would have guessed such thin cords could be so strong.

If not for Bryan and the kids, she might never get out of bed again. Janine resented their needs, their demands on her, and hated herself for that resentment. She was caught in a cycle that fed upon itself.

"Janine?" Bryan poured milk over Toby's bowl of cereal and handed him a spoon. "Did you hear me?"

Though she had tracked Bryan's movements, she didn't answer his question.

He went down on one knee beside her chair and took her hand. "I'm sorry," he said. "I should have realized it sooner. It's too much for you to take care of the boys right now. Maybe a few quiet days will help. A week . . . or two, even. Maybe that's all you need."

The pleading in his eyes begged for the words he wanted to hear, but she simply couldn't manage the effort it would take to say them. There was no point in it. There didn't seem to be a point to anything now.

Bryan responded to her silence with a sigh. After a moment, he stood to pull a yogurt-smeared Noah out of his high chair and walked toward the sink with his wriggling son held at arm's length. "My parents will be thrilled to keep the boys for as long you need, babe." Bryan pinned Noah to the countertop with one hand while he reached to wet a paper towel with the other. "I'll be back—Noah, sit still—I'll be back early this evening. I'm sure Mom will have lunch ready when we get there, but I'll start home right after we eat and the boys get settled in. I promise. You won't be alone after dark."

"Okay." The word breathed up her throat and past her lips, but she couldn't swear it was her voice she heard.

"If you're done eating," Bryan told Toby, "go wash up. And try to pee." He sat Noah on his feet and watched him toddle two steps before he plopped down. Bryan kept one eye on him as, once again, he knelt before her and took her limp hand in his. "Would you like to ride along? Maybe getting out of this house might be good for you." Again, he waited for a reply. Again, she gave none. He stood abruptly and ran his hands through his hair. "I just don't know, Janine. What's the right thing to do? Maybe I should call your doctor—"

A sharp burst of sound from her startled them both; her laugh had already rusted. "I'll be fine. Really."

Bryan, apparently not sure he should trust her judgment, stroked his bottom lip as he studied her. Finally, he forced a smile. "I'll have my cell phone on. You'll call if you need me . . . even if you just need to talk . . . or listen?"

She nodded.

"Hey, Tob," he called out as he picked up the baby, "you ready to hit the road?"

Janine stood and took a few steps toward Bryan. He extended Noah toward her, but she kept her hands pressed to her sides and only leaned forward to brush her lips across his plump cheek. Toby burst into the room and bear-hugged her thighs. She lifted a hand and gave his chestnut curls a perfunctory pat. When Bryan bent his head to kiss her, she forced her mouth to return the gesture.

"I'll be back before dark," he repeated.

She stood motionless in the middle of the kitchen, watching out the window as Bryan buckled the boys into their car seats, loaded their bags into the trunk, and backed down the drive. Her hand, hanging limp against her thigh, twitched a vague wave in response to his car horn's farewell honk.

"Come sit with me, Mommy."

Janine gasped and turned. "You startled me, Cara."

"Don't you want me here?"

"Yes. Oh yes, sweetie, I do. I just . . . didn't hear you come in." Janine forced a smile for her daughter. "I'm happy you're here." She glanced around the room, confused. "I . . . um . . . let me get a cup of coffee."

She faltered. "And . . . I should . . . I'll fix your breakfast." Cara, with her pale angel hair and clear sky eyes, was her golden girl. Her firstborn. Janine filled her cup, then slipped two slices of bread into the toaster. "Cinnamon toast, right?" She didn't listen for an answer. When Cara had a choice, she always picked that for breakfast.

Sunshine streamed through the bay window into the breakfast nook. "I should take you somewhere today," Janine said, but even before the toast popped up, she knew she wouldn't. She didn't have the energy. Though time alone with Cara was something she needed—something they both needed. Her little girl seemed so distant lately. Something was wrong. Janine hated the loss of closeness they had always shared. Depression had stolen so much of her life from her. Despite her desire to go back to bed, to sleep, to block everything out, she would resist for Cara's sake.

Janine carried her coffee mug and the toast to the table. She set the plate beside Cara's open book and took a seat across from her. "What's that you're reading?"

Cara lifted the book so she could see the title—*The Popcorn Club*.

Janine smiled. "That was my favorite book when I was a child. I must have read it a dozen times."

"I know," Cara said. She glanced at the toast. "I like oatmeal."

"But—" Children change. They grow up when you're not watching and one day they leave you behind. Tears welled and caught in Janine's lashes, but she blinked them back and got up to fix the cereal. As she stood at the stove, waiting for the water to boil, she watched Cara. Her eyes weren't tracking the words; she was only pretending to read. The pages lay unturned. Cara sat on the edge of the chair, her back rigid, and though her legs dangled, she didn't swing them as Janine had so often watched her do.

Janine poured the oats into the pan and stirred. Bryan was right; the children picked up on her mood. It affected everything. Despite the sunlight flooding the outside world, the kitchen seemed to reflect her inner darkness. She had to make more of an effort.

"You're very quiet this morning, sweetie."

Cara looked toward her but said nothing.

A few minutes later, Janine carried the oatmeal to the table and sat the bowl in front of Cara. When she ignored it, dread pressed down on Janine until she could breathe only shallow sips of air. She had sensed a shadow, some dark thing, stalking her for weeks. She knew her daughter. Cara's unusual silence this morning meant she was trying to find the courage to tell her something. And mother's instinct told Janine it was something she didn't want to hear. Something that might change their lives forever.

Janine sank into the chair across from her daughter. If she monopolized the conversation, if she talked fast enough, maybe Cara wouldn't be able to say the thing she didn't want to hear.

"What would you like to do today? It's your choice. Whatever you—"

"Are secrets good, Mommy?"

"Oh. Well . . . I guess some secrets can be good. And some can be bad. It would depend on what the secret is and why you're keeping it and who—" She stopped babbling and choked down a swallow of coffee gone cold. "Does it seem like a good secret to you?" The shadow deepening in Cara's eyes was answer enough. Janine mentally flipped through a stack of questions she didn't want to ask and settled on what she hoped was the least dangerous. "Whose secret is this?"

"It's mine," Cara said. Then she clapped her hands over her eyes and whispered, "And Daddy's."

No. She couldn't deal with this. Could not. The light in the kitchen seemed to narrow to a small circle in front of her eyes, then slowly expand until Cara sat exposed in a light so bright Janine's eyes watered. She squeezed her lids closed until tiny neon squiggles hid the afterimage of her child.

"Are you mad at me, Mommy?"

"No," Janine cried even before she opened her eyes. "God no. Why would I be mad at *you*?"

"Do you know what the secret is?"

"Oh. Well . . ." Janine shot from her chair and grabbed her cup and Cara's untouched bowl. Her vision blurred with tears as she stumbled to the sink. She set the dishes on the counter with a bang, sloshing coffee into the oatmeal. She leaned over the sink uttering a strangled moan, sure she would vomit any second. When that didn't happen, she stood upright and covered her face with shaking hands. But that posture only reminded her of Cara's whispered confession—*And Daddy's.* Oh, God.

For the third time that morning, Janine crossed the kitchen to face her daughter. She had no choice. Cara needed to tell her all. She would have to listen to it. She dropped into her chair.

"You can tell me, sweetie."

"Sometimes," Cara began, "when Daddy and I are alone, we play a game."

Janine listened to every word, though at times she looked away to give Cara the courage to tell all the painful, private, perverted things her monstrous father had done to her. During the moments Cara faltered, Janine gazed at the photos on the wall behind her. Family photos from happier days. For a moment, she wondered why she'd enlarged and framed the shot of Noah and Toby with . . . who? A friend's daughter? A neighbor's child? But then her eyes landed on the latest photo she'd added to the wall—a shot of Bryan and Cara, and she had to grip her chair seat to keep from jumping up and ripping it down.

Mercifully, Cara's recitation finally came to an end.

"Daddy told me don't ever tell anyone. You won't tell him I told you, right?"

With all her will, Janine pushed down the rage she felt toward Bryan. She rounded the table and knelt by Cara's side. "You're my angel.

I love you so much. Don't you worry about Daddy. He won't ever hurt you again."

• • • •

Hours later, when Bryan pulled into the driveway, Janine walked to the same spot in the center of the kitchen where he'd left her that morning. She stood the same way, with her arms pressed to her sides, her fists hidden in the folds of the nightgown she still wore. But instead of standing motionless, she now trembled with rage. She was ready for him.

He stepped into the kitchen and fumbled for the light switch. "Christ!" he yelled when the kitchen lit up. "Why are you standing in the dark?" He looked her up and down. "Has something . . . are you all right? Janine?" He started toward her.

"Stop where you are," she said. "I want to see your face when you tell me why."

He paused, still four feet away. "Tell you why? Why what? Honey, sit down. I'll fix you a cup of tea. Sorry I'm late." He stepped toward her again. "The traffic—"

"She told me."

Bryan stopped cold. "*She*? Told you what?"

"All of it. Every sick disgusting detail." She felt a little thrill as his look of confusion turned to fear.

"*Who* told you?"

"Cara, you son of a bitch. Your *daughter*."

His breath exploded from him as though he'd been punched. He shook his head slowly.

"Don't you deny it, Bryan. Don't you *dare* call her a liar. Give her *that* much." She was screaming now, and it felt good.

"No." He moaned. He shook his head harder. "She's . . . she couldn't—"

"Why? Because you told her not to tell? Told her to keep your filthy little *secret*?" She took a step toward him. He backed away. Her courage rose. "Wasn't it enough, *doing* it to her? Did you have to make her keep it locked inside too?"

Bryan made a choking sound. Janine thought he might be having a heart attack, but she hoped not. She didn't want him dead. Not yet. Not until he paid.

"Do you know what you did to her? Made her feel dirty and evil and guilty. You made *her* feel guilty!"

"Oh, God. I didn't do any of that. Janine, please—"

"Liar!" She moved closer to him. "She told me. She *told* me."

Again, Bryan reached out to take her into his arms. "Oh, honey, she couldn't have. You're confused. Something . . . oh God, something in your mind—"

The tears wetting his face only fueled her rage. As if it had a mind of its own, her right hand shot upward and then came down hard. The first blood spray, hot and sticky, shot across her face and into her mouth. She gagged. Her fury blazed white. Bryan gurgled as he tried to speak. She flailed and thrust and slashed. She hushed him. She made him pay.

Exhausted, she dropped her arm to her side and closed her eyes.

"What have you done?"

Janine swayed as she turned toward the voice. The room darkened for a moment, then grew bright.

"What have you done?" Cara repeated.

"I've taken care of it, sweetie. I've made sure Daddy never hurts you again." Then, she turned her head and, for the first time, saw the evidence of her rage. "Don't look! Oh, Cara, don't look."

"I'm not Cara."

"What? Sweetie . . . what?" She looked back at the little girl across the room. The white-blond hair, the blue eyes, the *Josie and the Pussycats* nightie. How did Cara even know about that cartoon? Janine's gaze shot to the photo on the wall, the one of the dark-haired children. The

Bryan clones, she'd called them. Not one of her children had her fair coloring. Not one.

And then she remembered.

Like a train of cruelty, each car a different scene flashing before her eyes, it all came back to her. Weeks ago? Months? A stranger had lured Cara away from her own front yard.

Three days later, he'd been stopped for speeding. Cara's lifeless body lay in plain view on the back seat of his car. Molested is the word Bryan had used when he told her. He had kept the details from her, but she knew. She *knew*.

Her sweet baby girl. Her firstborn. Her first dead.

Janine forced herself to look at Bryan's body again. Her mind cleared for the first time since Cara's death. Bryan had never touched their daughter except in the pure loving way a father should. What was it he had tried to tell her in his last moments? It was all in her mind? Yes. Oh God, yes. He hadn't known how true his words were. The prison where she kept her childhood memories had been unlocked—her mind unhinged—by the shock of Cara's death.

The little girl who had stood across the room, the ghost of herself, was gone now. Cara was gone. Bryan was gone. Janine stared into nothingness. Moments later, the knife clattering to the floor startled her back to reality.

"I killed the wrong daddy," she whispered. And then, she started screaming.

Your parents, if that's what they are, take you for the first Mandatory Suitability Review just after your fourth birthday. That one's not so tough. They ask you a few questions. You look at pictures and make up a story about them. They ask you to draw some objects. You're totally clueless at that age, so you hold back nothing.

Your second Review comes three years later. By then, you're used to evaluation at school. You know you won't pass to the next reading group, the next math level, the next grade unless you "perform to your potential." Still, you're a kid. People make allowances for kids. Right?

They give you a break after that—or you think they do—because your next exam is only physical. They don't schedule your next Review until you're twelve. By then you've learned a few things. Those judged become critical. Your nose and hands and feet have outgrown your body. Half the time, your brain refuses to function, and you feel stupid, so, of course, that becomes your go-to word. Stupid teacher. Stupid school. Stupid world. You even dare to say, "stupid Review," but you're scared this time. Really scared. You've heard things.

You passed, but you're not relieved because now you know more than you wanted to. They confirmed some of your suspicions by the exhaustive physical, by the questions they asked, by the pictures they showed you, by what they asked you to draw—but worst of all, confirmation comes from the four newly abandoned stations in your classroom.

They schedule you for Reviews annually from now on. You'd like to think nothing of the acceleration, but you know too much. You know they're watching you, studying you more closely now. And you can no longer fool yourself about the reason. This is the last decade of the twenty-first century—and you've entered puberty.

You endure school each day as if moving through a minefield. "Forbidden" becomes the mantra of your teachers and counselors. You complain to your parents, if that's what they are. "Just obey the rules," they say. All your instincts buck against those rules. "I can think for myself," you scream back. The next week, you're notified of transfer to boarding school. Non-coed. Four months earlier than normal.

You understand nothing and everything. You feel isolated now, yet you are never alone. All activities are supervised. Your every move caught on camera, every word recorded. You see a few friends from your old school, but you're all wary now. You exchange only trivialities verbally while speaking truth with your eyes. Their eyes scream fear. When you dare to face the mirror, your eyes reflect the same.

Your next Review is far different from the previous ones. No more stories and pictures. It's hardcore evaluation time—mind and body. You pass, but not by much, you think. Back at school, you force yourself not to look for missing faces around the classrooms and in the halls. But you can't ignore the empty bed next to yours in the dormitory. An old phrase comes to mind: *thinning out the herd*.

You intensify your efforts. All in vain. Midway through your fourteenth year, they send you home. They don't explain. You don't need to ask. They have judged you *nonessential*. For two days, you lie in bed feeling nothing. On the third, you get up and destroy everything in reach. You smash your entertainment module with a chair. You shatter your electronic tablet. You rip apart every tunic and pair of pants in your cupboard, creating a pile of gray tatters in the middle of your cubicle. Then you stomp on it and scream. No one stops you. You scream until you taste blood. No one cares.

On the fourth day, your parents, if that's what they are, flank you on the walk to the chamber door. You say nothing to them. You had a moment of panic, a moment when you feared you might give way to tears, to begging, but that's over. You've known too much for too long. You're numb now, appropriately controlled.

"Don't fight it," they say. "Just breathe deeply. It's easier that way."

"How would *you* know?" The words taste bitter on your tongue, but you have no spit to wash them away. You're a dry husk. You lied to yourself—you're not at all numb.

In the middle of the chamber stands a glass tube, six-feet high and three feet in diameter, with a door standing open on one side. The top of the tube is open too, but suspended above it is an apparatus, a domed cap with a hose that snakes down and over to a metal valve. A technician sits at the controls on the far side of the chamber. He doesn't meet your eyes. You step into the tube. The door closes. The dome descends.

You are fourteen years, six months, and ten days old, and it's eight minutes past the eleventh hour on the third day in the fifth month in the ninety-second year of the twenty-first century.

This was your existence.

On their twenty-seventh wedding anniversary, Teresa's husband gave her the biggest shock of her life. The evening started out perfectly. Derek had made reservations at their favorite restaurant. The new dress she'd bought for the occasion fit her like a dream, though she'd been a little disappointed that he hadn't commented on it. And it was a perfect October evening with a full moon and the crisp air scented by dry autumn leaves crushed underfoot.

As they perused the menu, they discussed the latest news from their children. She spoke of her misgivings concerning the next selection for her book club. He told her the rumors about a personnel shakeup in his firm. Then, as they sipped their wine, they lost themselves in thought as long-married couples often do.

Later, halfway through eating his steak, Derek looked up at her. "I can't do this anymore."

For a few seconds, Teresa thought he'd just announced his intention to become a vegetarian, but when he forked another medium-rare bite into his mouth, that self-deception disappeared quicker than chocolate at her Women's Society meetings. Finally, forced to acknowledge what her subconscious, call it female intuition if you must, had tried to tell her for months, she understood.

"I've met someone," he said as he chewed. "I want a divorce."

At least he could have delayed this conversation until after dinner. The sheer lunacy of that thought made her smile. For a few seconds, while he chewed and she beamed, their facade of celebrating a perfect marriage remained intact. Then Derek swallowed and reached for his wine glass. Subconsciously anticipating a toast, she automatically picked up her own. Then she snapped back to reality. She dropped her napkin on the table and stood.

"Here's hoping you regret this decision every single moment of the rest of your narcissistic, infantile, sorry excuse of a life, Derek." She deliberately tipped her glass and drowned his steak in cabernet.

For a moment, she relished the sight of him, dumbfounded, staring at his ruined dinner. Then she picked up her purse and walked out.

Her indignant stride faltered when she reached the parking lot. Derek had driven them to the restaurant in his car. A flush of humiliation marred her righteous exit until she remembered the spare key tucked somewhere in her purse. She dug around the bottom and zippered sections of it as she tottered on her heels toward the car.

"What a waste," she muttered, thinking of all the money she'd spent at the salon and on the dress and new shoes for the occasion. And then she felt the pang of realization that waste applied to more than just her attire tonight.

With her eyes focused on Derek's car, she kept her ears alert for his footsteps rushing up behind her. Her exit would be most satisfying if she could make a getaway and leave him stranded. She breathed a thank you when her fingers found the key.

Just before she drove out of the parking lot, Teresa glanced toward the restaurant and saw Derek burst through the exit. With a laugh, she gunned the engine and burned rubber. Why should she care? This was *his* car.

Teresa's jubilation died away before she reached the corner. Her marriage was over. This rough patch was one they would not weather. This she knew because she no longer cared to try. Derek's current lust interest was not his first. Always before, she'd been the one to swallow her pride, strangle her anger, and work it out. She'd simply refused to allow Derek's tomcatting to affect their marriage, downgrading it to no more than a kitten playing with the yarn in a knitting basket. It took patience, but it could be untangled, unknotted, made usable again.

Not this time. She was tired. Her fiftieth birthday was only two months away. If she didn't resurrect her dignity this time, she never would. Always before, she'd had their children to consider, but they were adults now, on their own. It was time to put herself first. It was time to hire a lawyer.

• • • •

In the eight months since, Teresa had often kicked herself for not divorcing Derek sooner. When the children, busy with their own lives, had taken the announcement of the breakup in stride, Teresa concluded she hadn't hidden as much from them as she'd imagined. But even that sobering realization had worked for the best. She discovered the freedom of living without secrets. She now faced each day with an energy she hadn't felt in years. Oddly, although she found a new enthusiasm for her future, she also found herself reexamining her past, recalling who she'd been before she met Derek.

Reminiscing with her old friend Kathy had helped. Teresa's high school experience had been an average one, some good memories, some bad. She had even kept in touch with some classmates for several years after graduation, but when Derek had taken the position at his company's headquarters, and they'd moved to Maryland, she'd eventually lost contact with them all except Kathy.

Teresa had met Kathy their freshman year, and they quickly became best friends. They even resembled each other, so much so that strangers assumed they were sisters. They'd drifted from that extreme closeness, as happens in long-distance relationships, but they were friends for life. Every few weeks they talked on the phone, but they emailed almost daily. In some of those messages, Kathy relayed updates on their old friends.

Teresa had ignored Kathy's first email about the high school alumni site. She and Derek had still been married then. *It's fun seeing what everyone's been up to*, Kathy had written. Now, here she was, on the phone, bringing it up again.

"You're missing out, Teresa!"

"On what?"

"Remember, Mark Peletier? Of *course* you do." Kathy laughed. "Well, he just signed up. You won't believe who he married after he and Diana divorced. And he's single again!"

Yes, she remembered Mark, but did she really care who he'd married and divorced? And besides, he still lived in their hometown, two thousand miles away. Didn't he?

She had a new life; she didn't need to resurrect the one she'd lived years ago. Decades ago. How pathetic would that be? Kathy could have fun with the alumni thing if she wanted to, but it wasn't for her. The kids and her interior design business were enough to keep her fulfilled. With a quick snap of a nod as if to confirm that to herself, Teresa wrapped up their conversation and opened her laptop. She had at least two hours work to do here and then several phone calls to make before she headed out to meet with a potential new client.

Ten minutes later, she minimized her work files and typed in the URL for the alumni site. She entered her info and added herself to the list of her high school graduating classmates. She even dared to add a photo, though it wasn't a close-up, and her face was partly shadowed by Derek, whom she'd cropped out. What could it hurt to join? It would be harmless fun. After all, most of these people lived hours away, even by air. They had no connection to her real life, nor would any of them want one.

She was wrong.

By the next morning, she'd received an email from Mark Peletier—and read it numerous times before daring to respond. His email simply said: *Hey, Teresa. Saw you'd signed up at the Collier alumni site. Nice to see another familiar name from my past.* That was harmless enough. She was just "another familiar name" to him.

She'd responded: *Hello, Mark. Yes, isn't it funny how seeing our classmates' names brings back a flood of memories? I hope you're doing well.* She'd automatically typed *Love, Teresa* but caught her mistake and changed it to just *Teresa*. It was better to keep these things merely polite.

He hadn't taken it that way. In his return email, he'd summarized his whole life since graduation. He'd even hinted that he hoped they could meet again sometime. What the heck was she supposed to do with that? She called Kathy and read Mark's email to her.

"Thanks a lot for getting me into this awkward position," she told Kathy.

"How is it awkward? You were in love with him . . . from a distance, sure, but now maybe you'll get your chance. And hey, he's rich . . . and still good-looking!"

Typically, Kathy had jumped to the furthest conclusion.

Teresa waited a full twenty-four hours before responding to Mark's second message. She briefly mentioned her recent divorce, but mostly she wrote about her children. It was safer to stay in neutral territory. They each had three children, though he had three sons to her one son and two daughters. Her son and one of his had played high school football, like Mark had, so they had that in common too. And, of course, they were each living alone now.

They exchanged emails daily for over two weeks, and then she didn't hear from Mark for several days in a row. Her disappointment when his name failed to pop up in her inbox shocked her. She supposed it was inevitable that he'd move on. How had he even remembered her? She'd been just one of eight girls at the next cafeteria table, flirting with the jocks.

On the fifth day of no email from Mark, she gave up, turned off her computer, and took her youngest daughter to lunch and shopping. Soon after Derek moved out, she'd realized how little of her life involved him. He'd worked so many hours for so long that most of her activities revolved around her children and friends. Still, she and Derek had shared a history. They'd grown up together in many ways, though apparently only she had matured. Then again, she'd been mooning over her teen heartthrob for weeks. How mature was that?

Late that night, she poured a glass of pinot grigio and checked her email. She couldn't suppress a smile when she saw a new email from Mark. He apologized for his absence—*dropping the ball*, he said. He'd made an unscheduled business trip, was in Japan at that moment, but would resume their *delightful conversation as soon as possible*. Her heart tripped at that point, then did a backflip when she read his sign-off: *Thinking of you tonight, as I have often in the last 32 years.*

Before she even got out of bed the next morning, she checked the world clock on her phone for the current time in Japan. It was fourteen hours ahead, almost 9 p.m. there. She rushed to her computer. She ignored all other email, opening the new one from Mark immediately.

Good morning, pretty lady, he'd written. *I fly back to the States in the morning, my time. I have to go to corporate in Atlanta for a day, and then I thought I'd check out Baltimore. Will you meet me for lunch on Friday?*

• • • •

By Friday morning, Teresa's hair was freshly highlighted and her nails perfectly manicured. She paced her bedroom trying to decide which of her two new outfits showed off her figure best. Thank God for her divorce; the stress had provided a permanent loss of the ten pounds she'd struggled with the last few years of her marriage. The pale aqua sheath won out because it accented her tan so well. She looked good. No, she looked great. Damned great.

She left home early. Two blocks from the restaurant, she pulled over to check her hair and makeup one last time and to slow her breathing. What impression would she make if she arrived disheveled and hyperventilating? She restarted the car, then sat for a moment wondering at her sudden insecurity. Yes, as a giggly girl, she'd had a crush on Mark, but life had tempered her in the years since high school. She'd raised three children, ran a small business, and—yes, she had—managed to keep a marriage solid for most of twenty-seven years. She was Woman and could roar with the best of them.

Teresa drove slowly, took her time parking, and sauntered into the restaurant, hoping she looked relaxed and carefree, which she only then realized was a waste if she'd arrived before Mark. But she spotted him, already seated. He'd been there awhile, judging by the empty glass the server had just taken from the table. She took a deep breath and followed the host toward him. "I'm sorry, Mark. I didn't realize I was late."

He rose but paused, a slight frown narrowing his eyes, before he smiled and took her hand. "You're not late. I was overanxious. You'll have a drink?"

"Chardonnay," she said to the server and took the chair the host had pulled out for her.

"Have you had work done?" Mark made a vague gesture at his face.

"Is that your way of telling me I look good *for my age*?"

"No, I didn't mean it that way. It's just . . ." He shook his head. "It's nothing. Though, of course, you do look wonderful . . . for any age." He flashed that charm-your-panties-off grin she remembered well.

Teresa laughed, or tried to, but it came out uncomfortably close to a giggle. Mark kept looking at her oddly, though he smiled each time she caught him. When the server returned, she practically grabbed the glass from him and took a sip that bordered on gulp. Forcing another deep breath, she transformed back into her real self.

With all this talk about her looks, she felt justified in assessing his. He had obviously attached to his alumni profile a particularly flattering photo of himself, taken a few years ago. He was still handsome, with a full head of dark hair, barely graying at the temples, and only a moderate thickening around his middle, but his face looked fuller than in his photo, a bit bloated really. She ought not to judge, though. Maybe the puffiness was only a side effect of his recent air travel.

After ordering, they launched into small talk. "How was your trip to Japan?"

"All work, no pleasure," he told her. "How is your decorating business faring?"

"Very well, thank you." *Now that I'm not distracted from it by a philandering husband.*

They sipped their drinks. She tucked one side of her hair behind her ear. He loosened his tie. The easy relationship they'd forged through email had disintegrated in person.

"Sitting here, actually talking to you is very different from emailing, isn't it?" he said.

"I was just thinking the same thing."

They lifted their glasses at the same second, then laughed and clinked them together, as if they'd meant to do that all along.

"Here's to a future that could be amazing," he said.

"I'll drink to that," she said. Mark had already emptied his glass and was signaling for another.

"You know what I remember most about you at Collier?" he asked. She raised her brows in response. "Those black flats you wore. Very sexy. I never forgot them."

"Really?" Why did she not remember those shoes?

"I used to check every day to see if you'd worn them."

Oh God, the man has a foot fetish. Could she live with that? She tucked her feet under her chair.

"It was cute, the way they showed just the top of the separations between your toes. Very sexy."

Yep, definitely a foot fetish. Good thing she hadn't skipped the pedicure. Still, it made her uneasy that the stroll down memory lane had become so personal before they'd even finished the appetizer.

"What I remember," she said, "is how much food you guys ate for lunch."

"Hey, ours was the varsity team table. Coach worked every one of those calories off us at practice." Mark grabbed the Scotch from the tray before the server had a chance to set it down. "And all you girls were always on those crazy diets. Even the nerds ate healthier."

Oh, right, anyone who hadn't been a jock was a nerd. "Bill Gates was a nerd," she said, not meaning to.

"What?" He knocked back his drink. "Oh. Yeah. Well, I've done all right for myself too. And Gates never got crowned Prom King." He winked at her as if they were sharing a dirty joke.

The server brought their entrees, and Mark ordered another drink and a bottle of chardonnay for her. "No, thank you. No more for me."

He frowned at her. "You're not turning into Polly Prude on me, are you?" He held up a hand. "Oh, right. Someone might recognize you here. It wouldn't do for little Ms. Businesswoman to be seen letting her hair down in public."

Teresa caught the glances from diners at nearby tables. Mark's voice had grown louder with each whiskey. The kitchen staff would be able to hear him by the time he finished the next one.

He leaned toward her, as though he were about to whisper, but his volume didn't change. "You sure didn't look like a prude in that tight red sweater."

"Red sweater?"

"You know the one." He winked at her again. "But what was wrong with your other nose?"

"What are you *talking* about, Mark?"

"Never heard of anyone getting plastic surgery to make their nose bigger." He lifted his glass in the general direction of her face. "And you've capped that tooth." His head wobbled as he shook his finger at her. Unfortunately, that finger was connected to the hand that held his glass, and he sloshed alcohol as he wagged.

Black flats? Red sweater? Smaller nose? Teresa stared at him, perplexed. Then she remembered a red sweater—on Kathy, who'd sat across from her at lunch. Kathy was the girl with the smaller nose, peg incisor, and black flats. "I'm afraid there's been a mistake, Mark."

"They screwed up your order? Probably a bunch of damned foreigners working in the kitchen." He lifted his hand to signal to the server, but she pulled it down.

"No, it's not the food." Teresa laid her napkin on the table and scooted back her chair. "*You've* made the mistake, Mark." She picked up her purse and stood. "It wasn't *me* you've 'thought of often for the last thirty-two years.' It was—" She caught herself, inventing a name on the fly. "It was Polly Baker who wore the red sweater and black flats."

"Aha." He nodded. "*That's* why you look different. So, hey, you wouldn't have Polly's email address, would you?"

Teresa glared at him for a moment, then leaned down to look him in the eye. "No. I don't. But don't bother looking for her. Your dream girl is, and always was, a lesbian." She straightened, then spoke at a sound level to match his. "I'm sorry to hear Viagra doesn't work for you, Mark. Maybe the doctors will come up with something else . . . eventually."

For the second time in a year, Teresa lifted her chin and stalked out of a restaurant, leaving a poor excuse for a man behind. She vowed never to be so weak again. Her life was good. She certainly didn't need a man to fulfill her. All in all, she'd learned a lesson cheaply. Some people are better left alone.

Nina stared at her full coffee cup with no memory of having poured it. If only she could sleep. Even four hours straight would be heaven. Her prolonged insomnia now endangered her safety and that of everyone around her. She probably shouldn't be trusted to operate household appliances. And she certainly shouldn't drive, yet who would do the shopping if not her? Certainly not David.

"Speak of the devil," she muttered as her husband entered the kitchen.

"Hm?" He arched his brows, but his eyes only skated across her face as he headed toward the coffeemaker. "You remembered I have a business dinner tonight, yes?" He filled his travel mug but not a cup for home. He remained standing. "So, how did the new pills work?"

"They didn't."

"Well, give it a couple of nights." He straightened the suit coat he'd folded and draped precisely over his forearm and then picked up his mug. "What's this new medication called again?"

"It's Somniou, and I've already taken it *five* nights, David."

"Oh," he said, a frown not quite registering on his Botoxed forehead. "I'm sorry; I didn't realize."

"Time flies when you're having fun."

His mouth twitched in a semblance of a smile. "I know it's been a nightmare"—he paused, fingers against his lips—"sorry, poor choice of words. I know it's been a rough four months, but you have to *believe* this new medication will work, Nina." He leaned down to kiss her goodbye. "I'll call you later."

Her hands gripped her cup to keep them from grabbing his designer tie and dunking it in her coffee. How sweet that would be. The smile he witnessed as she turned her face up to his had nothing to do with adoration, but his vanity would never allow that to cross his mind. Of *course* she loved him. Of *course* she worshiped his every breath. Didn't everyone?

At the door, he turned. "If you should be asleep when I come home, I'll try not to wake you."

Nina waved him off and took a sip of coffee. Why did she even bother? Despite an abundant intake of caffeine every morning, the fog no longer lifted. She spent her days on autopilot. Yesterday, she stood in front of the mirror, searching for some tiny movement behind her eyes. An electronic blip. She listened, head tilted, eyes closed, sure she could hear a nearly imperceptible whir of hard drive. Was she really Nina? Or had David—Mr. Perfection—traded in his real wife for the Stepford version? After all, robots don't need sleep, do they?

"And thoughts like that will get you locked up in a psychiatric ward, Nina." She left her cup sitting on the table and went in search of her walking shoes. More exercise and sunlight, her doctor insisted, would reset her circadian rhythm. The tone in Dr. Lertona's voice told her he no longer had confidence in his prescriptions, medicinal or otherwise, but she played along. What else could she do?

It was April, an altogether gorgeous time of year in the San Joaquin Valley. The sun warmed her face. A breeze played with her hair. She sauntered along, down one block, over two, down three, passing roses the size of saucers in a myriad of hues. Passing cats and cars and other walkers—some with dogs, some with partners—she smiled, or nodded, or said hello, like any normal woman fresh from a full night's sweet sleep. How easy it was to pretend.

• • • •

I seem to be in a park, walking on a path, headed toward a bench. Who is that man? I know him, or I think I do.

He sees me and stands, smiling. "Nina," he says, taking my hand. He motions for us to sit.

I know his voice. His gaze is tender. When he smiles again, it's slightly crooked and crinkles appear at the corners of his eyes. Laugh lines. I love this man.

"I'm so happy you've come back," he says.

"John?" I say. "You're John Cusack."

His eyes well up, but he laughs. "Of course I am." He leans forward, and placing a hand behind my neck, he pulls my mouth to his. His kiss is soft and sweet, gossamer, like cotton candy. "I love you," he says, "but I'm worried about you. You're sleeping too much."

"Am I?" My eyes are heavy. He's fading. John slips away from me.

Nina lay in the dark, eyes open, thinking of the dream she'd woken from. Why John Cusack? She hadn't seen any of his movies lately. He hadn't been on her mind, yet he'd evidently been in her subconscious. He reminded her of . . . someone. Someone important to her. But "sleeping too much"? Hardly. She closed her eyes. If only she could fall asleep again. Maybe he would return.

Three long, sleepless hours later, the alarm sounded. David woke and began his stretches. "Never get out of bed without stretching first," he often told her. Often. And like everything else he said, he expected her to see the wisdom in it and follow his example. She never did.

"I had a dream," she told him.

He sat up and started his neck rotations. "Well then, congratulations; that means you slept." Down and up to the left, hold, one-two-three. Down and up to the right. "At least for a while." Chin to chest. Face to ceiling. Gentle moves. Let the weight of your head do the work. "Obviously, the new medication is beginning to work."

"I slept for an hour. At most."

"Don't be negative, Nina." He stood to finish stretching.

She got up and went into the bathroom, partly because she had to pee, partly to piss him off. The master bath was supposed to be his privilege first in the morning. He would count the seconds she delayed him.

She would make sure it was at least thirty seconds longer than it needed to be.

After David left for work, Nina took a morning walk. For good measure, she walked again in the afternoon. While she stood on the patio grilling chicken that evening, she watched the sun setting. As rose dimmed to periwinkle then darkened to indigo, her blood effervesced with anticipation. She would sleep tonight. She would dream. That assurance made it hard to sit through dinner and their evening routine.

"I think I'll go to bed now," she said and laid her book aside. It was barely nine. David switched off the television. Not a good sign.

"I'll join you," he said and winked.

She endured the delay in getting to sleep by pretending to make love to John Cusack instead of David. He was none the wiser. She wondered if he ever had to stop and search his memory for her name. If she went missing, would he have to consult a photo to describe her to the police? During dinner, a question had danced on her tongue, *Why, exactly, did you marry me, David?* Although to be honest, if he'd reversed the question, she couldn't have answered it. Even the recollection of their wedding was lost to her now. Their life together seemed faded. A once-favorite shirt, the life washed out of it.

• • • •

As soon as I round the bend in the path, John comes into view and rises from the bench, smiling. How did he know to watch for me? Oh! I remember now; we arranged this meeting. We meet often at this time, in this place. How silly of me to forget.

"Nina, my love." He wraps me in his arms, a fierce, yet gentle hug. My cheek presses into his collarbone. A sensation both familiar and strange.

"I can't remember—"

"Shhh." John pulls back and, with a finger under my chin, tilts my face up to his. "Concentrate on now. Hold on to it." He kisses me. A brief, eternal kiss.

"I thought of you all day," I say.

"I think of you always. I watch while you sleep, waiting for the moment you wake and come to me. It's never soon enough. You never stay with me long enough."

I'm crushed to learn I've caused him sorrow. "I'm sorry, John, please—"

"Why do you go back there, Nina?"

His eyes search my face. I feel his longing.

"Do you not love me any longer?" he asks.

For just a second he looks like . . . like . . . Tony? He has tears in his eyes.

"Oh, John. Oh, my sweet John," I say. "Don't you know I love you with all my heart?" My vision blurs. My mouth goes lax. "John?" I mumble. Is he still here?

"Stay with me." He grasps my hands, frantic. "Don't sleep!" he cries. "Can't you see you're falling asleep again?"

• • • •

"What did your doctor say?" David asked as they ate lunch in his favorite pretentious gastropub.

"He asked how the new medication was working."

"Don't be pissy, Nina. Of course he asked that, and you told him it was. Did you tell him about the *dreams*?"

She hadn't. "It's normal to dream."

"Well, it's not normal to sleep half the day *hoping* to dream." He slapped a palm against the table, rattling the glassware. "I *knew* I should have gone to the appointment with you."

"Please, don't make a scene, David." He calmed down immediately, as she knew he would. Heaven forbid, David Manrieght lose control in public.

"It has to be the medication that's causing these bizarre dreams." He took a sip of wine, drying the rim with a surreptitious wipe of his thumb as he set the glass down. But she noticed. She always noticed.

"I don't think they're bizarre. They seem so real."

"Even so, Nina, dreams are *not* reality. They're only your subconscious speaking. Instead of sleeping your life away, you should seek the services of a psychiatrist who could put you in touch with your subconscious more effectively. I happen to golf with an excellent one." Another sip. Another wipe. "I'll talk to him this afternoon."

"There's no need. I don't care about the dreams anymore."

"So you won't be napping this afternoon?"

Nina didn't respond. She only stared at the toad that had hopped onto David's plate during his lecture. He gave no indication he noticed. She didn't bring it to his attention.

• • • •

On her afternoon walk, Nina saw another toad. Not likely a mere coincidence. Add toads to her list of things to watch out for. She'd taken to avoiding rose bushes, which made her route more complicated, but since their scent had turned to one of rotted meat, what else could she do? Pet walkers were another necessary avoidance. If one took her by surprise, she dashed off to hide behind a hedge or car or porch chair until they were out of sight. Her safety demanded such measures. Some people had no respect for how easily Komodo dragons could snap their leashes and attack.

David had kept his word. Just as Nina finally dozed off for her nap, the receptionist for a Dr. Shawkees called to tell her they'd scheduled her an appointment for the following Tuesday—six days away. Angry because the chirpy woman had snatched away her dream time, Nina uttered a curt thank you and hung up. David had overstepped. A new plan was in order.

Thirty minutes, at least, passed before she fell back to sleep.

John waits, as always, on the bench. I try, as always, to sneak up on him. But he senses my approach long before he could hear my footfalls on the cement path. His face lights up, as always. He takes my hand and we walk. I often stay long enough now to make it to the bridge over the swan pond where we stand and talk.

"I'm thrilled with your progress," John says. The breeze lifts a strand of my hair over my eyes, and he brushes it away with a touch that's feather light for such a strong hand. "You're going to come back to me for good soon."

"Why did I leave?"

His eyes are shadowed as he looks into mine, and though his mouth quirks into a smile, it too is melancholy. "That's something you'll discover in time, Nina." His fingers entwine in my hair and his lips brush my forehead.

"Please, don't let me leave," I say. "Why can't you keep me here?"

He wraps his arms around me. "I try. I always try."

The heartbreak in his words squeezes me as tightly as his arms, yet before I can respond, I feel the breeze swirl around me and know he is gone. I am gone.

• • • •

Nina didn't trust the psychiatrist, Dr. Shawkees. Except for the dangling Victorian earrings he wore, which didn't even match, he was David's twin. The doctor asked her a few questions to which he already knew the answers. She was no fool. David had told him everything. So she said what the doctor wanted to hear and left the first session with a new prescription. That was all that mattered.

She wasn't surprised when David pulled up beside her just as she reached her car in the parking lot. No doubt, the doctor had phoned him while she stood at the receptionist's desk scheduling her next appointment, which she had no intention of keeping.

"Get in," he said. "We'll go to lunch."

She ought to have questioned David about the rusted lime green convertible he was driving. Instead, she eyed the man in the passenger seat. "I don't know him," she said.

"Of course you do, silly. He's Fred Flintstone."

She backed away, shaking her head. "I'll drive my own car."

David shrugged. "Yabba dabba do!" He gunned the engine and drove up and over the parked car blocking his way out to the street.

Nina watched, her mouth agape, forgetting for a moment that she was supposed to follow him. David had lost his mind.

By the time she got to the restaurant, David had already ordered for her. "I'm sorry," he said, "I'm due in court in forty minutes, and I feared you were running late."

She sat down.

He poured a precise three ounces of chardonnay into her glass. "So, how did it go?"

"Well . . . you know . . ." She took a sip.

He sighed. "No, Nina, I'm afraid I don't know. Please, elaborate. You *did* discuss your sleeping problems, correct?"

"You know very well that Dr. Lertona faxed my medical history to your psychiatrist friend." She buttered a piece of her roll. "So there was no need to rehash that."

"But you discussed the dreams?"

She motioned for David to wait until she chewed the bread. He would have given her *the look* if she'd talked with her mouth full. She swallowed. "Of course."

"And?"

"I made progress on the dreams. And he prescribed a different medication."

"Good." David sat back, relaxed. "I think that will help."

She smiled. "I'm sure it will."

When their food came, she couldn't eat. Potting soil covered everything.

· · · ·

On Wednesday, Nina slept most of the day. Without walks. Without pills. She'd mastered the technique. Six glorious hours talking with John . . . well, minus the time it took her to reach REM sleep—only minutes now. They'd crossed the bridge and walked in the rose garden. It had been heaven.

She watched the clock throughout dinner with David and then their evening routine, counting down the minutes until she could go back to bed. Sleep necessitated a double dose of pills that night, of course, but David, expecting her to take one, was none the wiser that she'd secreted an extra capsule in her palm.

"You're looking fit," he said as she set her water glass on the bedside table. "It must be all the walking you're doing."

"I suppose." She hadn't walked for over a week. It was far too dangerous. The neighbors spied from behind their closed blinds with their weapons aimed at her. That morning, tired of waiting to catch her on the street, they'd blasted away part of the kitchen. "I can't make you coffee in the morning," she told David. "The coffeemaker was atomized."

"Oh, that's no problem," he chirped. "I've decided to drink belladonna tea from now on." He ruffled his feathers and tucked his head under his wing to sleep.

"That will poison you," she said, but he was beyond hearing. So be it. He was no longer a concern to her anyway.

· · · ·

The next morning, David filled his travel mug with coffee, then poured another half cup and sat down at the table with Nina. "I wonder . . . do you feel up to a weekend away?"

"Where?"

"Remember the bed and breakfast we loved so much in Pacific Grove?"

With her cup to her lips, she only murmured. She had no recollection of visiting the place. So many memories lost. And, suddenly, as she half-listened to David's reminiscence, she understood why.

"I'll take tomorrow off," he said. "We'll drive over in the morning." He reached across the table for her hand. "I think it will do us both good to get away for a few days."

Tomorrow. Nina smiled. It was time.

After David left, Nina sorted clothes and started the laundry. As each load washed, she straightened the house, vacuumed, and dusted. She scrubbed the kitchen sink, counters, and floor. She cleaned the master bedroom and bath last. With all the clean clothes folded, she packed David's travel bag, zipped it closed, and set it on the floor of his closet. She carried his shaving kit into the bathroom and set it on the counter between the double sinks so he could add his things in the morning.

Satisfied that she'd remembered everything, Nina went to the kitchen. She poured herself a glass of wine, brim full, and carried it out to the patio. She sat in the sun, sipping it slowly. For the first time in months, she could think. The mind was marvelous and terrifying, idly twisting reality like a lock of hair, while focused elsewhere. Now, she'd awakened and recognized true love at last. She rose from her chair.

Inside the house, she stopped in the kitchen for more wine before returning to the bedroom. She set her glass on the bedside table and stepped into the bathroom. Ten pill bottles lined one shelf of her medicine cabinet. Each time a prescription failed, Dr. Lertona had switched her to another. She set the bottles—some half-full—on the counter and opened them. One by one, she poured them out. Blue and pink and yellow, alongside the new purple ones Dr. Shawkees had prescribed.

Nina cupped her hand against the counter edge and scraped the rainbow of pills into it. She carried them into the bedroom and sat on the bed. Washing them down with wine, she swallowed the pills two or three at a time. Then she lay down to wait.

• • • •

"Where are you?" I can see nothing but white. Cold and clammy white. It's silent. Oh, God! I was wrong. John's not waiting for me here. Something dark in the mist moves toward me. I whimper as it grows closer. "Please . . ."

A hand breaks through, reaching toward me.

My eyes open again.

"I'm here, Nina," he says.

He's sitting in a chair beside the bed, clasping my hand. I pull my gaze away from him to look down at myself. I'm dressed in a coarse cotton gown. I scan the room. Institutional chic. I'm in a hospital.

He leans closer, looking into my eyes. "You're really here, aren't you? *Really* here this time."

"Yes." My voice is raspy, unused.

Tears well in his eyes, and he pulls me closer until our foreheads touch so I can't see him break down. He chokes out one word. "Stay."

He holds me while he gets his emotions under control. I wait until I think he can answer my question.

"Why am I here?"

"A new prescription for your insomnia . . . you . . . a bad reaction. They revived you, but . . ." He clears his throat and takes a deep breath. "You've been in and out."

"How long?"

"Eleven days."

"I thought this was a dream. I thought you were John Cusack."

He laughs. "You always did see a resemblance, but it's just me, Tony."

"My husband."

"Yes."

"This is my real life?"

"This is your real life. And I am the man who loves you very much."

On the wall at the top of the stairs is the face of a gorilla. *It's not real*, Daddy says, *you're just making it up out of shadows in the bumpy paint*. I'm still scared of it. I have to take a big breath, close my eyes, and run all the way up and past it into my room. I shut the door to keep it out.

But I'm not really safe in there. My room is really scary now because I'm alone at night. My sister isn't in the bed beside me. She's in the hospital. I don't know where that is. I've never been there. It's where they take sick people. Maybe the gorilla made her sick.

One night, when I woke up in the dark, I saw a lady in a white nightgown standing at the end of my bed. I whispered to her, but she wouldn't talk to me. When I crawled down to touch her, she wasn't there. She scared me. I told myself it must be Mommy. But in the morning, I didn't ask her how she disappeared like that. Maybe it wasn't Mommy. It might be the gorilla tricking me.

I live in a house of secrets and shadows. Most of the time, I don't talk to anyone about them. No one talks to me about them either. I'm only six.

And I'm a bad girl.

I know this because my mean uncle told me I'm not a lady. He said, *your voice is too loud, and you gulp your food, and when you're wearing a dress, you sit with your knees up, showing your panties*. I'm a bad girl, and that's why I see scary things.

My Aunt Ginny—not the aunt who's married to the mean uncle—is staying at our house now. She calls me Kitten. She dressed me like a ballerina for Halloween. She doesn't know I'm not a lady. Aunt Ginny takes care of me because Daddy and Mommy are at the hospital all the time. My aunt reads to me. I love books. There are no scary gorillas or sick sisters in the books she gets from the library.

I make pictures for her. I drew a grave in the rain. She frowns when she looks at it and pulls me onto her lap. *This is a very sad drawing*, she says. I tell her, *it's just a remember of Grampa's funeral.* She hugs me a long time. *Don't worry about your sister*, she says, *Cathy will be all right.*

I want to believe her, but she has that look on her face, the one like Daddy and Mommy have when they come home from the hospital. I hear Mommy crying at night. Daddy hugs me a lot, but he doesn't talk.

Come sleep in my room, I say to Mommy and Daddy and Aunt Ginny. They all say, *No.* They don't say why, but I know. They're scared of the gorilla. It's a lie when they say they can't see it. They know it's going to get into my room because I'm bad. No one can stop the gorilla. But no one says that. We don't talk about secrets and shadows in our house.

Justin Tisserand slumped in the leather club chair in front of the television, watching the prerecorded episode of *Focus America*. Lauren smiled at him. Tanned and blond—aglow with life—her face filled the screen in high-definition glory. Only Justin's knees, wedged against the ottoman, kept him from sliding to the floor. He clutched a crystal decanter in one hand and a glass in the other, but on this day, the ninth day of a binge, the Scotch had lost most of its punch. It still intoxicated him, but it no longer deadened his pain. Tears ran freely down his cheeks.

A voice roared outside his alcohol-fumed bubble. Who's it was, he had no idea and didn't care. His misery wanted no company. The light of his life had been snuffed out, leaving him isolated in darkness, blessedly unreachable, except by that damned roar—again. This time he couldn't block it out.

"I *said*, turn that damned thing off."

Justin peered up at his father, slowly comprehending the order, but before he had a chance to obey, his father stalked to the home theater system. Lauren's image disappeared. The old man turned to face him, his upper lip curled in disgust. For one drunken moment, Justin imagined his father as a silver-haired Elvis impersonator in a custom-tailored suit.

Raymond Tisserand had a presence that intimidated nearly everyone. Only a few men commanded his father's respect, and Justin was not one of them. Just the weight of his father's glare compacted his vertebrae, pushing him down another inch into the cushions. His father ruled both his family and his business in every sense of the word. It came as no surprise that he was also a commanding force in the country's textile industry. *Focus America* would have done an episode on him eventually, even without the "phenomenon" angle. But like bloodhounds on the trail, once their so-called investigative reporters caught the scent of scandal, they focused their klieg lights on it, tore it open, and zoomed in for a close-up.

Justin moaned as Lauren's face flashed in mental rerun.

"I'm ordering you to snap out of this . . . this *funk* you're in, Justin. If you need help, Weller will prescribe something, but you *will* get back to work. Do you hear me?"

"I hear you."

His father snatched the decanter from Justin's hand, emptied the last of the whisky into a glass for himself, and settled into the chair opposite his son. A piteous smile, as phony as it was chilling, flitted across his lips just long enough for Justin to know the indomitable Raymond Tisserand was about to change tactics.

"Son, I'm not trying to make light of your feelings. I've had the same experience and—"

"I know that."

"Well . . . yes, of course you do. So you should know how much I sympathize."

Justin had caught the almost imperceptible upward twitch of his father's lip again. No doubt sympathy was the last thing the man felt.

"I know it's hard, Justin, but you have to pull yourself together. Life does go on. Even when you don't want it to."

"It wasn't supposed to be—"

"Yes, it was, son, I just didn't know that. How could I, for God's sake?"

"*God* had nothing to do with it." Justin pushed himself halfway to a stand before the force of his father's glare crumpled him back into the chair. Fascinated, he watched as his father roared another command through clenched teeth.

"Don't you dare criticize our heritage!" Raymond emptied his glass and stood, towering over his son. "When have you ever *once* bemoaned the privileges our success has provided you?"

"I'm supposed to feel privileged? *Privileged*. God." He made it to his feet this time, standing face to face with his father, but only for a moment before he swayed.

As Justin lost eye contact, Raymond grabbed him by his shoulders, forcing him to sit again. "Listen to me. This has thrown you off kilter, and that's understandable, but there is too much at stake to let you continue like this. You're a grown man. You have responsibilities. What's more important, you're a *Tisserand*. That entitles you to great rewards, but it also obligates you to observe family tradition. I will not allow you to continue this display of ingratitude. It's . . . dishonorable."

Hatred lay bitter on Justin's tongue, but fear kept him from spewing it out. Silently, he watched the old man take a step back and slip his concerned-father mask on again.

"You've paid your debt, son—our debt—and now we can move on." Raymond crossed the room, pausing at the door to add, "I'll tell Weller to stop by in the morning."

Justin held back a smirk until his father left. Adam Weller, the family physician. The family puppet. His father had pulled Weller's strings to avert more than one scandal. According to Dr. Weller's reports, a severe case of the flu, not a fistful of Klonopin, had nearly killed his sister six weeks ago.

And then Lauren ... died.

The ingenious Dr. Weller had explained away Lauren's death as the result of injuries suffered during a seizure. Her medical file now contained records documenting previous seizures. The doctor had doctored his files. Justin had no doubt a substantial amount of money had changed hands for that deception. Nothing but the best for the Tisserand family. He closed his eyes and folded into himself with a sigh.

"And now we move on." Like a good Tisserand man. Like his father had moved on after his own wife's death, the mother Justin knew only in photographs. His father had followed the example—the tradition—of generations of Tisserand men before him. "Just pay your debt and get back to work. Life goes on."

And life *would* go on. Just maybe not the way his father expected. If they hadn't already, *Focus America* would air an update.

"Can your threats or payoffs stop *that*, Dad?" Suddenly more sober than he'd been in nine days, Justin retrieved the remote control. Though *Focus* had interviewed his father and filmed him at work and home, they aired very little of that footage. That had all been a smoke screen. They had already decided to zero in on Lauren. Justin clicked the remote and her face once again filled his view.

The camera switched to the still-friendly-at-this-point correspondent Paula Barrett. "You know what I want to ask you," she said.

Lauren laughed. "Of course. You want to know if I lose sleep wondering if I'll be the next Tisserand wife to die young."

"Well . . . do you?"

"Never. I'm a healthy woman. I expect to live to see my great-great-grandchildren born."

"But not all the victims of this phenomenon died of natural causes," Barrett said. "Edward Tisserand lost two wives mysteriously, Clara in 1918 and Analise in 1926."

"I hardly think this one tragic aspect of the family's history deserves the label 'phenomenon'. And it certainly shouldn't outweigh the abundant love and joy we share." Lauren beamed. "This is an unusually close-knit family."

"Some people wonder if that closeness is meant to hide something," the reporter said.

"We have nothing to hide . . . except maybe a few trade secrets. The unfortunate women you've asked about died of different causes, none of them unexplained."

"You deny that more than one death was suspicious?"

"More than one was *accidental*," Lauren said, "but there was nothing suspect about any of them. If you take the deaths in context of their era, the causes were actually quite common: catching a heel in the hem of a long dress and falling; postpartum infection; possibly a suicide resulting from untreated depression. What's mysterious about those?"

Barrett shot her an exaggerated look of disbelief. "You find nothing suspect in the fact that your husband's mother, grandmother, great-grandmother, great-great-grandmother, and so on—seven generations of women—*all* died suddenly, and the oldest of them was only twenty-seven years old? You don't find that a little odd?"

"I haven't studied the histories of other families; I don't know if that's odd or not. But I do know that if this family was not so well known, so successful, no one would even consider their deaths noteworthy, let alone cite them as evidence of some *phenomenon* at work."

Paula Barrett promised "more of this fascinating story" and the program went to commercial.

Poor Lauren. Such sincerity born of ignorance. On the day that interview was taped, Lauren, staunch defender of the family's honor, had finally refused to answer further questions about the deaths of the Tisserand wives. Instead, she offered to lead the television crew on a tour of the family estate, ending with a walk on the beach near sunset.

Clips of that tour opened the next segment of the program. In voice-over, Barrett named each of the "victims" as the screen zoomed in on their portraits hung throughout the house. Elaborately framed oil portraits depicted the first three wives.

"In 1802, Henri-Paul Tisserand's teen-bride Mary Catherine is *said* to have died of childbed fever, what today would be diagnosed as a streptococcal infection. The death in 1832 of Elizabeth, wife of André Tisserand, was *attributed* to blood poisoning. René Tisserand's wife Marie Barbara died in 1863, *supposedly* after she tripped and fell down two flights of stairs, breaking her neck."

The next four wives were shown in photographs, sepia-toned giving way to hand-tinted. Barrett's voice continued her roll call, her tone casting doubt on each cause of death.

"Adaline Tisserand, wife of Pierre-Paul, was the first of the wives found dead on the beach below the family property. Known to be aqua phobic, her death in 1891 was *declared* a drowning, though no explanation of why or how she got into the water was ever given. The next mysterious death occurred in 1918 when Clara, the first wife of Louis Tisserand, died after *accidentally* ingesting an unidentified toxic substance. Louis remarried after the death of his and Clara's son, an only child, at the age of five. His next wife, Analise, died in 1926 when she fell from her horse, *apparently* the second of the Tisserand wives to die of a broken neck. In 1953, Josephine, wife of Edward Tisserand succumbed to chronic dysentery . . . according to the *reported* cause of death."

As Wagner's wedding march played in the background, the camera swept down the main staircase of the house and through the hall to the dining room, stopping at last on the leaded windows that overlooked the rose garden where Paula Barrett stood alone, her head bowed. A studio photo of Justin's mother flashed on the screen followed by a quick succession of film clips: the bride, the socialite, the new mother. After a fade out, the camera, now in the garden, focused on Paula again.

"On a Saturday afternoon in mid-June of 1982," she said, "Raymond Tisserand married Jeanine Coleman here in the formal garden of the family estate on Kenewamscot Bay. In February 1988, barely five months after the birth of her son, Justin, Jeanine either fell or jumped to her death on the jagged rocks along the shore below the family estate. According to her physician, Dr. Adam Weller, she was under treatment for postpartum depression at the time."

The next shot showed Lauren and Paula strolling on the beach as Lauren gave a reverent account of the historic "stone by stone" down-river move of Henri-Paul's original home and its considerable expansion at its new location above the bay. The two women stopped below the cliffs at the far end of the property.

"We're standing in a significant spot, aren't we, Lauren?"

For a moment, Lauren frowned, then her eyes widened and her jaw set, as she understood the point of Barrett's question.

With a tilt of her head, indicating sincerity as false as the sympathy in her voice, Barrett moved in for the kill. She gestured to the rocks below the cliff. "Isn't this the very spot where the ravaged bodies of your husband's mother and great-great-grandmother were found?"

Something flickered in Lauren's gaze. Standing among the crew on the beach that day, Justin had interpreted that flicker as just an indication of Lauren's anger, but watching the film now, he wondered if he'd been wrong. Could she have had a premonition? Did a flash of understanding followed by fear fuel the torrent of four-letter words Lauren flung at Barrett and the television crew? Justin had watched Lauren struggle to compose herself.

"This is a wonderful family," she said. "The Tisserands have nothing to hide, nothing to be ashamed of or to apologize for. Henri-Paul Tisserand arrived in this country a poor young man with a dream. He founded a dynasty, if you will, and there's a wonderful story there. Why don't you '*focus*' on that?"

Only an edited portion of Lauren's response made the final cut, of course. From the studio set, Paula Barrett had ended the show with a question. "Is it possible the recent near-death experience of Raymond Tisserand's daughter, Judith Tisserand Randall, is connected to this, as yet, unexplained phenomenon?"

Justin switched off the television and said, "Oh, yes, Paula. It's possible. It's very possible."

His sister, Judy, had married Cary Randall nearly two years ago. One day, about six weeks earlier, their father had taken Judy aside and let her in on a secret—the secret of the family's success, though Justin didn't know that at the time. Later that night, Judy swallowed all her little blue pills.

Their father summoned Dr. Weller. Judy recovered from "complications of the flu" and one evening soon after, while doped into a near zombie state, she did her heritage proud by descending into the maze of cellars below the house with Cary and returning without him. Fifteen minutes later, a cobwebbed and dirt-smudged Cary stomped into the family room announcing that he did not, in the least, find Judy's "little game" amusing.

Justin thought it funny until he noticed his father's reaction. Never having seen that look on his father's face, it took days before Justin put a name to it. Raymond Tisserand had been terrified.

Justin was only bewildered. He had no clue what really happened between Judy and Cary that night or why they packed up their eight-month-old daughter and flew to London at dawn the next day. His father spoke to no one about it; he spent hours pacing the house and muttering to himself.

Soon enough—too soon—Raymond enlightened Justin.

One month after Judy's suicide attempt, Raymond summoned his only son, his second-born child, into his study. "Pour yourself a drink, Justin. Pour us both one."

His father's enormous mahogany desktop lay hidden under books and charts. Though he had seen it only once before, Justin recognized the topmost book as the journal written by Henri-Paul Tisserand, their immigrant ancestor, the man who had started it all. Silently, Justin toasted his fifth great-grandfather with a sip of Bourbon. As the top-shelf whiskey slid smoothly down his throat, he took a closer look at the mess on the desk. He grinned when he recognized the chart unfurled beneath the journal as the family tree.

"What's this all about?" he asked, gesturing toward the desk. "Have you discovered the Tisserand skeleton in the closet?" With one glance at his father's reaction, Justin's amusement evaporated.

"Sit down, Justin."

Feeling as though he were a life-sized version of one of the lead soldiers displayed on a table across the room, Justin obeyed. Instinct told him his attempted joke would be his last for a long time.

Raymond stood for a moment, staring into his drink, before he dropped into the chair behind the desk. "Henri-Paul left Boulogne in 1795 with only his mind, his health, and a dream. He came to this country virtually penniless. He even lost his name. Did you know that? Some ship's clerk or immigration officer mistook his occupation as his surname. Anyway, once the misnomer had been officially recorded, he was stuck with it."

Of course, Justin knew about the name change. He had heard the family history recited his whole life, but he wasn't about to interrupt his father to say so. The old man was not himself tonight, and whoever he was petrified Justin.

"I didn't know, you see? By miracle or chance, until now, the first-born has always been a male. So I thought—" He stared at Justin for a moment, then rose and walked to the fireplace, to stand with his back to his son. "I was wrong. She didn't want Cary."

The seeming nonsense of his father's words shook Justin out of his silence. "Judy? Are you saying Judy wants to divorce Cary? But they just went—"

"Henri-Paul was apprenticed as a weaver, and he learned the trade well, but he had ambition and he had the intellect to match. Before long he—"

"*Judy*, Dad. What about *Judy*?"

His face a mask, Raymond turned to Justin and continued his speech in monotone. "Henri-Paul wrote in his journal that for weeks he had seen in his dreams a powerful waterfall with a mill built above it, and he set off to locate the falls. 'drawn to it like an arrow' he recognized the land immediately, though it surprised him that no one had laid claim to it. He scoffed at the ignorance of the nearby townsfolk when they told him the land was cursed, but he took fair advantage of both their superstition and their need, buying the acreage and the water rights for a pittance.

"While he camped on the land, he drew up the plans for his mill. In his words, he 'sought inspiration and guidance from the land, and she provided all'. In record time, he raised the capital and hired men from Boston to construct the mill, company store, and worker's dwellings. Many of the builders and their young women found jobs in the mill that soared three stories above the falls. Soon after it went into production, Henri-Paul took a fifteen-year-old mill girl as his first wife. The Tisserand dynasty had begun."

Justin had only half-listened to his father's recitation. Forced to memorize the legend of Henri-Paul Tisserand by the age of seven, the only reason he could think his father would waste his time repeating it now was that he had lost his mind. Maybe a blood vessel had burst inside the old man's brain. The glaze over his eyes lent weight to an insanity diagnosis. Justin wasn't sure his father even knew who he was speaking to right then.

"Are you all right, Dad? Do you want me to call Dr. Weller?"

His father shook a fist at him. "I want you to shut your mouth and pay attention!"

Justin sat frozen as the old man crossed the room to refresh his drink, though he hadn't yet taken a sip from the first pour. His outburst seemingly forgotten, he stared again into the amber liquid, silent for so long that Justin thought his father had dismissed him. Not daring to speak, Justin cleared his throat.

His father lifted his head. In the same flat voice, he continued as though there had been no interruption. "Above the entrance to the finished mill was a plaque engraved with the new family motto: *Le succès exige le sacrifice.* Success requires sacrifice. Henri-Paul's mill was successful. Very much so. Throughout the years, none of the problems common to the industry affected the family business. No fires, no supply shortages, no labor strikes. Not even war forced us to close. Nor have we ever dropped production due to market fluctuations. Our business sailed through the Great Depression as if it never happened. Success after success after success. So it was for Henri-Paul, and so it has been for each of his heirs. Successful beyond reason some would say, and yet—there has always been a reason for our success."

Raymond Tisserand turned to his son, his lips stretched into a mockery of a smile, and when he spoke, his tone reverted to the one Justin knew well. "Success is a bitch. That, my son, should be the real family motto. She's a jealous, greedy, fanged, clawed, bona fide bitch. One hundred and eighty-seven years ago, our renowned ancestor courted and won her—for a price." He lifted his glass in salute to the man in the portrait above the fireplace, "Congratulations, Henri-Paul." Then he downed his drink in one gulp.

Justin's mind screamed at him to run before his father continued his speech. *Run, before you hear something you will never be able to erase from memory.* But he couldn't move. Fear of his father's wrath paralyzed him.

"That damned *Focus America* report called her a phenomenon. When your grandfather gave me the same speech I'm giving you, he called her Tradition. In his journal, Henri-Paul called her simply '*la dame du succès*'. Call her what you like. You may hate her at first, Justin, but you will adjust. You will accept. We all did. In the end."

Justin's subconscious had already skipped forward to read the end of this tale, but his conscious mind refused to listen to that horrible conclusion. *This has nothing to do with me*, he screamed silently, and still he could not block out his father's voice droning on.

"When she didn't accept Cary, I feared we had done something to offend her. The last few weeks have been hell for me, but finally . . . I found the answer. Henri-Paul promised her the *wives*, you see. She craves only the fertile vitality of our women. The exchange is not made for the spouse of the firstborn child, but for the spouse of the firstborn *son*."

Raymond grinned with delight, as though he expected congratulations on his discovery. Justin saw only his father's madness. The man was a total raving lunatic. Had to be. Oh, dear God, he had to be.

• • • •

Now, twenty-two days later, at the sound of approaching footsteps, Justin switched off the television again and looked toward the doorway expecting his father's second assault of the evening, his second demand to pull himself together, to get back to work. Instead, the nanny entered, bringing his son to him for a goodnight kiss. Fresh from his bath, smelling sweet as only a two-year-old can, Noel reached out his chubby arms, wriggling for the nanny to set him loose. Justin's breath caught in his throat when he looked into his son's face—a face so closely resembling Lauren's.

The future heir of the Tisserand fortune, unaware of his debt to the Lady of Success, wrapped his arms around his father's neck. "Mommy's gone," he said. But he did not cry. Life goes on.

"I love you, Big Boy. Want me to tuck you in?"

"Read puppy book?"

"Sure. Anything you want. Go with Nanny. I'll be right up." Justin set the boy on his feet and watched as he toddled toward the door. Just before he passed through, Noel turned back to him and smiled.

When Noel's smiling image faded into Lauren's, reminding Justin of the last image he had of her, he finally manned up. He faced the truth. As they left the wine cellar that last night, Lauren had turned to smile at him—just before he pushed her into the dark side passage and locked the door. Just before she met Tradition and secured the future success of the Tisserand family business, Lauren had smiled at him.

Justin shook the image from his mind. With a sigh, he deleted the *Focus America* episode from the DVR. As his father had predicted, Justin had stepped up and accepted his family obligation. He had loved

Lauren, but when faced with the choice—not a *real* choice, actually—he loved his net worth more.

Elise tried to picture Colin as she drove toward the cafe. A few months ago, when he started leaving comments on her blog as Anonymous, she'd imagined him equal to any of *People* magazine's "Sexiest Men Alive." She kept expecting him to ask, like others had, why she never posted any photos of herself. But he never gave any hint at all that he was interested in what she looked like. So it seemed logical to assume he didn't want her to ask about his looks either. And she didn't. But she lowered her expectations of his to average Joe.

Sometimes she played a game, imagining her reactions to finally meeting him and discovering he was morbidly obese, hideously scarred, physically disabled, the nerd king, or just plain butt ugly. Then she chastised herself for even caring about his looks. His comments on her blog revealed him as witty, intelligent, compassionate—all things that mattered to her—yet, in her weaker moments, she focused on the formless shadow behind his words.

Into her posts, she slipped mentions of how the humidity affected her hair, or the percentage of people with different eye colors, or how she hated to find the last of a desired item pushed to the back of the top grocery shelf where she couldn't reach it. Something—anything—to elicit a snippet of personal description from him. She learned that he had curly hair, hazel eyes, was taller than average, and his first name was Colin. At least she had those details.

In a desperate measure, she invented and then disparaged a conversation among her friends sitting at Starbucks rating the men as they walked in. He commented that he hated the same game played by his friends. Though he understood the law of natural selection, he said, the people he held most dear in his life were those who would likely be passed over in such a shallow, primitive process. From that statement, she reasoned her estimation of average looking might be too generous.

Then Colin used the contact form on her blog to say he would pass through her town in two days and asked if they could meet. He knew a cafe by the little art gallery on Becker Avenue. Did she know it? She did and agreed to meet him. I'll wear a purple shirt and sit at a table outside, he told her, so you'll recognize me.

And now, she was only two blocks from the cafe, turning the corner, spying a parking spot up ahead.

Elise pondered why he hadn't asked how to identify her. Had he offered her an out? Had he suspected her to be shallow after all? Had he feared she would turn away, pretending she had no idea who he was if his looks didn't meet her standards?

She parked her car and looked across the street. All the tables on the cafe patio were visible from this angle. Most of them were occupied, but at only one sat a violet-shirted man. At the urgent pressure in her chest, she expelled the breath she'd held since spotting him. All the variations of Colin she'd imagined flashed before her. She'd got one exactly right.

In her mind's eye, she saw herself at home, dressed for this meeting and standing before her full-length mirror, examining her sallow, spotted skin, the thirty extra pounds she carried, and the lank mane that grew oily within an hour of shampooing.

So.

Elise started the car and headed home. She'd delete her blog. After a while, she'd forget the thrill of anticipating each of his comments. She'd forget she ever knew a man named Colin. She'd forget that she had pictured him perfectly the first time.

I'm not perfect, but I'm a good mother. My children deserve my best, and they get it. Always. Today, we're on my bed pretending it's our pirate boat. The kids are giggling because they know what's about to happen. Their laughter delights me more than any other sound, and I do what I can to hear it often.

"It's coming," I whisper. The kids press against me, squirming in anticipation. "It's getting closer. Watch out!"

The shark leaps into the boat, greeted by those piercing squeals peculiar to the very young. Alas, our beagle knows nothing of the role of shark, and she only wiggles and licks and yips, inducing a fresh round of hilarity before growing tired of our game and jumping off the bed. I fall back against the pillows, and my breathless children pile on top of me. You can't buy moments like this.

One by one, my little pirates roll off me. We lay side by side for a minute as if we're going to nap. No way. This is Chad's day off. I sit up. "Okay, kiddos, let's get Daddy to take us to Pizza 'n' Play."

"Yay!" Kaylee, Brandon, and Jade chorus.

"Get your shoes on and brush your hair." I maneuver over bellies and limbs to stand. "Kaylee, help Jade. I'll go find Daddy."

I look for him in his two usual Sunday places—in front of the TV or in the kitchen—but he's in neither. He's in the garage. "What are you doing out here?"

"Just straightening up things."

"Cancel whatever plans you made for this afternoon."

Chad stares at me for a moment before he frowns. "Why?"

"Because"—I smile as I move closer and wrap my arms around his neck—"I'd like us to take the kids somewhere."

He sighs. "You already told them we're going, didn't you?"

I bite my lower lip and look up at him wide-eyed. He's always been a sucker for my feigned innocence, particularly when I'm dressed in nothing but a bit of black lace, so I bait him. "If we tire them out today, sexy man, they'll go to bed early tonight."

"Tire them out where?"

"Pizza 'n' Play."

"Aww, Beth. It's *Sunday*." He pulls my arms down and steps back. "That place will be packed."

"But that's what makes it more fun for the kids."

"Right," he says, "for the kids."

"So are we going?"

He sighs again. "Of course. Give me a minute to wash up."

Just as we get all the kids rounded up at the door, I remember I have bread rising. "Get them in their seats," I tell Chad and head for the kitchen. *Shoot.* The dough is ready to proof, so I have no choice but to punch it down, cover the bowl, and shove it in the refrigerator. We'll have a slow-rise artisan loaf instead. As I wipe the olive oil off my hands, I glance out the window to the driveway. Kaylee and Brandon appear buckled in, but Jade sits on top of the van, holding up her shirt while Chad blows raspberries on her stomach. Her laughter carries through the closed window, making me smile. He's great with the kids. Why does he balk at the activities I plan?

"Hey, Mommy," Brandon says when we start down the street, "you know what song I want to sing?"

"Noooo!" Kaylee clamps her hands over her ears.

"Sing," Jade says, clapping.

"All together now." With a wink at Brandon, we begin, "*This is the song that never ends . . .*" It's a fifteen-minute drive to Pizza 'n' Play, and long before we arrive, I've climbed back to sit beside Jade so I can reach behind me and tickle Kaylee into giving in and singing along. Eight is a difficult age. She's cultivated the sophistication appropriate for a third grader, but it's only a thin veneer over the uncensored abandon of childhood. I wish I could make her understand that adulthood lasts forever. There's no need to rush toward it.

We've talked about our childhoods, Chad and I. His was happier than mine, and yet he's pushed it far behind him. He's disconnected from his inner child. "Somebody has to be the adult in this family," he informs me when he's in a bad mood. I tell him he's missing out on a lot of fun. He's growing old too fast.

As far back as I can remember I wanted to be a mother, and not just any mother. I wanted to be a great one. I've always known that I'd be a room mother, scout leader, coach, whatever it took to be involved in my kids' lives to the fullest. There was never a question that I'd be a stay-at-home mom. I want my kids to have all the advantages I didn't have—the music, dance, swim lessons, the camps, the teams, the social clubs. I want to give them everything they need, and most of what they want.

Our lives are busy, chaotic, noisy. I love it.

• • • •

Chad plays with Jade in the toddler section, while I alternate between Kaylee and Brandon's activities. I'm sure she would just as soon I stay with her brother, but I refuse to let our bond weaken. After forty minutes or so, Chad catches up with me and hands over Jade.

"I'm going to order the food," he says. "There's an empty table back near the pinball machines. Grab it."

"Order healthy, Chad."

For a second, he just looks at me. Then he shakes his head as if I've said something beyond comprehension. "This is not exactly a haven for sprouts and whole grains, Beth. We all need a little junk food sometimes."

"Wow, Jade," I say as he walks away, "is Daddy a little uptight or what?" I round up Brandon and Kaylee. We claim our spot and wait. Chad, now standing in the pick-up line, is texting someone, and that sets my teeth on edge. If he tries to rush through our family time so he can drop us off at home and go watch the rest of the game with the guys, he can forget any favors from me tonight.

Chad returns with what passes for a veggie pizza here. I blot the grease with napkins, knowing that he's giving me that look again, so I don't protest the root beer he ordered. The kids, of course, are thrilled with his choices.

Barely ten minutes later, Brandon swallows his last bite of pizza. "Can we have dessert?"

"Later," I say. "What should we play next? How about the tunnel maze? Jade can do that with us if I help her."

"Are you staying here, Daddy?" Kaylee asks. He nods. "Then I'm staying too, Mom."

"You can't just sit," I tell her. "We're here to *play*."

"I'm tired."

"Daddy, tell her how much fun she'll be missing."

"Beth," he snaps, "do you *ever* consider that others might have wants or needs different than yours?"

I shrug. "All right, Kaylee. Stay here, but you'll be sorry." I finish my lunch and then pull out the wipes to clean messy hands and faces while Chad takes the trash to the bin. "Come on, Brandon and Jade, my fellow fun lovers."

When the three of us exit the third tunnel, we're overlooking our table, and I see the real reason for Kaylee's plea of *tiredness*. She and Chad are eating ice cream. Despite my quick effort to urge Brandon forward, he sees them too.

"Hey, they're eating dessert *now*."

I shoo him forward. "You'll get ice cream when we finish the maze." Jade whines for *scream* the rest of the way through the tunnels. Why must Chad always undermine my rules?

"You could have waited for us," I tell him when we return to the table with our cones.

"Is the chocolate good, B-man?" he asks Brandon. "I almost got that."

"Strawberry's best." Kaylee's tone dares her brother to argue.

"Stawberry bess," Jade cries, though she's eating vanilla. She holds up her cone to Chad, and he licks the drips running down the side. Brandon notices and raises his cone for me to taste. I sigh, letting go of today's little disappointments, and take a big, fat swipe.

Brandon follows up his "Mom-meeee!" with such a dramatic pout that even he has to laugh with us. We're a happy family, having a good time, and that's what today is all about.

Jade hands the mushy nub of her cone to Chad, and while he wraps it in a napkin, she grabs his cell phone. He takes it out of her hands, wipes it off, lays it on the table, and begins cleaning the vanilla smears off her face. The phone's screen lights up with a text notification. I grab it.

An odd thing happens when I see the message. I read the words, but comprehension lags a second behind.

Hey, lover, don't cancel on me. I neeeeed you!!!

Chad snatches the phone out of my hand, but he can't remove those words from my memory. I will see them forever. Slowly, I meet his eyes. There's a message in them I can't decipher. His lips move, but I hear nothing. In the midst of a jam-packed, chaotic Sunday afternoon at Pizza 'n' Play, I'm surrounded by silence. Set apart. Distanced. Diminished. Discarded.

The silence is more real than I am. In those few seconds, I realize it's been there for a while. I just never heard it. Maybe I refused to listen. Now I'm alone with it. Consumed by it.

And then the dings, blips, clangs, squeals, and chatter flood back. Life continues.

"Mommy Mommy, more scream," Jade says.

"Can we *leave* now?" Kaylee asks.

"Noooo," Brandon wails, "I only got to ride the helicopter once."

Chad looks away.
I breathe. In. Out.
I hear and hear and hear.
And I know.
There is no sound more devastating than the silence in noise.

• • • •

Dear reader, thank you so much for reading these stories. If you enjoyed them, please tell a friend. Word-of-mouth praise is an author's dream. And I would be delighted if you left a brief review at your favorite booksellers' site.

About the Author

Linda Cassidy Lewis was born and raised in Indiana and now lives with her husband in California where she writes versions of the stories she only held in her head during the years their four sons were growing up. She lives in the city and is thankful for the gift of imagination that whisks her away to sea or mountain or countryside whenever she wishes.

To stay informed about Linda's future book releases, please subscribe to her mailing list[1]. And she loves hearing your thoughts about her books, so please connect with her online.

Website[2]

Facebook[3]

---

1. http://eepurl.com/u6zkv

2. https://lindacassidylewis.com

3. http://www.facebook.com/lindacassidylewis

Don't miss out!

Visit the website below and you can sign up to receive emails whenever Linda Cassidy Lewis publishes a new book. There's no charge and no obligation.

https://books2read.com/r/B-A-ZXVH-GLGCC

BOOKS 2 READ

Connecting independent readers to independent writers.

Also by Linda Cassidy Lewis

A Bay of Dreams Novel
The Brevity of Roses
An Illusion of Trust

A High Tea & Flip-Flops Novel
High Tea & Flip-Flops
Love & Liability
Open & Honest (Sometimes)

Edgewater Love Series
Building Love
Midnight Love

Standalone
The Silence in Noise and Other Stories

Watch for more at https://lindacassidylewis.com.